EARTH'S DAUGHTER

EARTH'S MAGIC BOOK 1

EVE LANGLAIS

CHAPTER
ONE

IN A WORLD WHERE THE WITCH TRIALS NEVER HAPPENED AND magic was allowed to flourish...

The latest batch of lemon cupcakes, frosted with cream cheese icing, awaited my finishing touch. I took a deep breath as I prepared to—

Achoo!

I sneezed.

We're not talking a ladylike squeak either. I uttered a god-awful spit-and-snot-flying exhalation that practically shook the windows of my treat shop.

Big or small, didn't matter, the spray ruined my tray of desserts. My nose tickled again. I turned away even though it was already too late. I went into a good fit that left me with my eyes streaming and my nose sore. Leaning on my forearms, gazing upon the contaminated goodies, it occurred to me that only one thing could make me lose it like that. Something banned from my shop. Heck, I'd omitted it from my life with various cleaning methods that involved bleach and some pretty epic air cleansers.

A glance upward at my industrial ceiling with its ducts and pipes painted a lovely sky blue showed a moldy rag—not mine—with all its allergen spores, hanging over a light fixture. Confirmation of sabotage. The second time this week.

And the last.

Never mess with a witch. A lesson most bullies—and pests—learned at a young age. Even nice witches like me had their limits.

I didn't have a chance to retaliate until later in the day near closing time. Only then did I draw a hex on the snotty cupcakes with some leftover icing. Once they all bore the same symbol, I waved my hand over the tray and muttered a few words. They glowed green for a second as the spell set. The visual evidence of my trick faded before I grabbed the tray of ruined treats and headed for the back door of my shop. It opened onto an empty alley. The previous homeless occupant, Ralph—who'd worn a sign during the day and claimed the dead would soon rule the Earth—had disappeared a few weeks ago.

I'd have worried more if I'd not seen him taken by the Second Chances van. The town—with much encouragement from residents—had taken a bold stance on getting rid of the homeless, not by killing them as a slag paper hinted at but by having them rounded up and force-fed the help they needed—even if they opposed it.

It caused a furor in a small vocal group that claimed it went against their rights; however, after three months, the evidence became too clear to ignore. No more needles in the park every morning. No dodging human waste on the sidewalks or being accosted by aggressive panhandlers for change. Not one of the beggars I'd offered food had appreciated it over cash, Ralph being the exception. Each night I used to bring him some leftover treats, and if I had none, then I made him something just to make sure he ate. Maybe now that Ralph had been taken off the streets he'd get the regular meals and care he needed to get healthier. Safer.

My hip hit the bar to release the catch on the rear door. The alley itself had only one light over my door, barely enough to illuminate. An overturned crate allowed me to climb and hold the tray over the dumpster, which was full of bags but not much of a rotting smell. The vermin inherent in every alley near a restaurant ensured no food went to waste, and that included paper wrappers that smelled yummy.

I tilted the tray and watched the morning's work fall in a rain of lemony sweetness. It wasn't long before tiny green paws emerged to snare the cakes. Goblins took up residence after Ralph left. Which I didn't have a problem with. The issue started when they decided they didn't want to wait until the end of the day to be fed. They'd also mistaken me for a pushover. I might be sweet as my peach pie, but I didn't let anyone, or anything, take advantage of me.

As the goblins munched the cupcakes, uttering happy little grunts—the biggest one casting me sly and smug looks—I counted in my head.

Five, six...

Wouldn't be long now. Goblins weren't the only ones who could pull pranks.

It began with a belch, followed by many startled squeals, then much agitation as the mottled-skinned goblins suddenly exploded from the bags of garbage. However, there was no escape. One by one, they turned into the cutest little furballs.

Giant, jewel-like eyes blinked at me. Cuddly bodies begged for a squeeze. I just wanted to hug and squish them. I refrained and instead smirked.

"Oops. Did I accidentally hex the cupcakes to make you into the cutest version of you that you could possibly be?"

The lead furball with a slight scar amidst the fur over an eye, shook a fist at me and chattered.

I arched a brow. "Don't you dare give me attitude. We had an arrangement. I feed you leftovers at the end of the day, and you keep my dumpster rat free. You broke the deal."

It uttered a few clucks and high-pitched whistles.

"It's not permanent. *This* time," I warned. "But if it happens again..." They'd find out why they shouldn't mess with a daughter of the Earth.

CHAPTER

TWO

THE REST OF MY DAY PASSED EASILY. THERE WAS A STEADY stream of clients for my baked goods and just as many for charms. After all, my shop wasn't called the Hexed Cupcake for nothing.

As a witch with an affinity for Earth and all things that grew, I could hex pretty much anything that had once grown in the ground, which was to say most things, barring meat. Plants being the easiest for me.

Hence why I baked. Ingredients came from growing things. It proved easy to add a spell to the final product. Draw it in icing and then activate. Easy peasy carrot cupcake squeezy.

I offered the gamut of options to those looking for a magical kick. My green tea macarons for relaxation. Red velvet cupcakes frosted with chocolate for a quick orgasm—very popular with the sex addicts after their Thursday night meetings. My strawberry scones made a person ooze goodwill and happiness. I had many a nervous suit come in looking for that extra boost as they went to ask for a raise. The gamblers usually walked away with a PB and J cookie for good luck. Unlike some other witches with a talent for Earth magic, I only sold benign hexes, which meant no love spells and nothing to cause harm.

And before you accused me of doing bad things to the goblins, the shape change would wear off within a day and cause no lasting harm. The Becalm Hex was most often used to soothe rampaging animals, turn them from roaring beasts to cuddly pussycats. Or in this case, from green, bratty menaces to cutesy furballs. For some reason, the goblins hated this, possibly because I tickled the leader under its chin and cooed, "Who's the most adorable squishy ever? I could just hug you and love you and call you George."

With a squeak of terror that widened its big emerald eyes, the transformed goblin dove into the bags of trash with its crew.

That brought a smirk to my lips. They'd think twice before messing with me.

Despite the goblins' bad behavior, at the end of the next baking day, I still bagged the leftovers for them. While many might dislike them for their mischievous pranks, I knew if I could win their loyalty, they'd protect my shop against intruders and bad vibes. A gut feeling said I'd need that help.

Something big and bad was coming. I'd seen it in the patterns left behind when I'd dropped a bowl of raspberry puree on the floor. A murder scene of fruit that almost made me cry. After all, my bushes sacrificed giving me those berries, and I'd wasted them. A tragedy that had me saying a little prayer. *Dear Earth Mother, take these delicious seeds back to your bosom that they might one day flourish most bountifully.*

Exiting into the alley, I grimaced at the darkness. The bulb over the door had burned out. Again. Pity our town didn't have any Electro Witches. Better than a solar panel, I'd heard, and cheaper, too. They were in high demand, though, given they held the title for ecofriendly electrical solutions. One Electro Witch could charge several large-sized batteries a day! Even a minor one could charge a lightbulb so that it lasted for years.

I dropped the bag of leftover goodies into the dumpster to happy squeals. I didn't peek because I could only imagine the carnage that icing would cause, especially if the spell hadn't yet worn off from yesterday. Fur and buttercream did not mix well.

The rear entrance to my shop swung shut with a heavy thud. It took me three tries in the dark before I locked it and headed for the entrance of the alley. It ran straight through to a road running parallel. Despite the early evening hour, the streetlights shone, giving me something to guide my steps in the somber alley. The occasional car and truck whizzed by, traffic lighter at this hour than in the daytime.

I'd lucked out buying my shop, having picked it up when prices were still cheap before the area began to gentrify, or so they called it. Basically, it meant

cleaning up storefronts and bringing in young profes-
sionals and the striving-to-be trendy who loved
quaint shops within walking distance. Some might
lament the fact that those same people pushed out
those of lower social economic status. It did unfortunately happen, yet at the same time, it removed much
of the crime that used to make it at times hazardous
walking home at night. It left people like me conflicted
because, on the one hand, I wanted to help those in
poverty, but at the same time, I liked not fearing the
dark.

As if to mock that thought, a figure blocked the
end of the alley, and I paused. While the town had
been cracking down on violence of late, it still existed.
As a woman, I had to be extra careful.

I took a few steps forward, watching intently to see
if they'd move, so focused I never saw the bird that
swooped toward me.

"*Caw,*" it yelled as it passed in front of me in a rush
of feathers and a stink that had me swinging my arm
wildly.

Nasty crow. We'd had issues with them scavenging
for scraps. Distracted, I realized I'd not only gotten
close to the alley exit but the person blocking it hadn't
retreated. We were within a few paces.

I shoved a hand into my bag, my fingers seeking
the Don't-See talisman I'd bought from a stone witch,
the jade infused with a hex to turn away the glance of
strangers on the street. Given the figure appeared to be

staring right at me I could only assume the magic in my talisman required a refill.

I tried to maintain a firm tone as I said, "Excuse me, but could you please step aside."

The person stood statue-still. Didn't reply either. My hand slid from my bag to dig into my coat pocket for a different kind of charm. While I chose not to do harm, I would protect myself.

I pulled out a chunk of valerian root, known for its sleeping aid properties and again asked, "Please move."

"Ungh." The low moan raised the hairs on the back of my neck, and yet the stench that wafted had me taking a step back.

Someone needed a bath. Possibly some bleach. And those clothes? Definitely required a flame thrower.

Passing close by to the person didn't seem wise. I'd leave via the front of my shop to avert trouble. I spun around and headed for the rear door, only to hear the shuffle of steps as the person followed. A sign they looked to cause trouble.

I dug into my pocket with my free hand and gripped my keys. Would I have time to unlock the door? With my shaking hands, possibly not. I glanced in the direction of the other end of the alley. Farther away, but once I got close to the next road, I could yell for help. My pace increased, taking me past my shop's rear entrance and into the darkest part of the alley, where the crow suddenly swooped again.

"Caw."

I flailed madly as its wings beat about my head and found myself suddenly quite concerned about it pecking at my flesh.

Crows don't eat people. A reminder that did little to slow my racing heart.

I'd stopped walking during my mini battle with the avian offender, and a glance over my shoulder showed the other person close behind, an ominous bulky shadow that had yet to speak.

Run or stand my ground? A fight with my valerian root needed proximity. My magic usually required ingesting or touching for it to work, an unfortunate aspect, especially in a situation like this where my safety was compromised.

As the person neared, I held up my hand with my sleepy sprig. "Stop. Don't come any closer."

"Ungh." A moan emerged as the figure halted less than a pace from me. While the alley might be dark, I could see a face, clean shaven, the head bearing a short stubble, the eyes wide. A stranger— No. I recognized the face despite the lack of hair and beard.

"Ralph? Is that you?" It appeared like him, and yet didn't. Not only had he lost his wild mane and facial hair but he wore a clean two-piece scrub suit, pants a light blue and the shirt baggy. His feet were bare. His milky gaze stared blanky.

"Gaa..." He breathed the syllable, the stench of it unbelievably foul.

"What happened to you?" I whispered. He'd never

looked this unhealthy while living in my alley. He needed help.

I reached for him, and his hand shot out faster than expected to grab me by the wrist. His touch icy cold–and wrong.

So wrong.

I shuddered and tried to pull away. "Let go." In all the time Ralph was my neighbor he'd never laid a hand on me. Never done anything aggressive.

This Ralph didn't appear to hear me and uttered that groan again, "Ungh." The exhalation gagged me. Something was really wrong with Ralph.

I slapped the chunk of sleepy root to his face, boosting its innate somnolence properties with magic. A normal person would have immediately hit the ground snoring.

Instead, Ralph tried to bite my hand. I snatched it away just in time as his teeth slammed shut.

"Ung. Ung." He grunted and clacked.

My concern mounted, and I yanked at the wrist he held. His grip remained firm.

"Let me go, Ralph. You know me. Remember? Mindy." I tried to appeal to the gentle man inside.

A man that no longer existed.

As my panic mounted, rescue came from an unlikely source.

Tiny furballs of cuteness, and a few green-skinned, less adorable goblins, suddenly swarmed Ralph. The dumpster critters came to my aid and sank their sharp teeth into the hand and arm holding me.

Finally, a reaction. Ralph's fingers spasmed and released but only so he could grab a goblin and bring it to his mouth.

My lips rounded in horror as he chomped.

The caught goblin squealed.

"No!" My exclamation didn't stop Ralph from killing an unlikely rescuer. And by killing, he ate the poor furry goblin whole.

"Run!" I yelled when Ralph flailed his arm while reaching for another. The writhing wave of critters jumped, hitting the ground and bolting as fast as they could. With protection in mind, they climbed back into the dumpster. In a panic, I sprinted past the dumpster for the door to my shop, clutching my keys in a sweaty grip. I fumbled them, looking for the right one.

Jangle. Wouldn't you know I dropped my keys.

Instinct had me dodging as Ralph reached for me. I whirled to see him, mouth slick with blood and fur. He eyed me with violent hunger. I needed to protect myself, and yet, I had no weapon. My valerian root had been my only defense.

The choice came down to fight by hand or—I glanced at the dumpster—hide.

I ducked Ralph's next clumsy swipe and shoved at his midsection. He stumbled off balance, and I sprang upward to grab the lip of the dumpster and heaved myself up. Before I'd managed to clamber over the lip, Ralph grabbed my satchel. I twisted my head to let it fall off as I hoisted my butt over the rim of the garbage bin. I yanked the cover down and hoped the obviously unwell Ralph would go away. Or at least come to his senses.

He didn't.

Thump.

Thump.

Thump.

He pounded on the side of the dumpster hard enough it dented. I knew because I felt it dimpling under my spread palms. Luckily, it didn't occur to him to climb in with me. But at the same time, he didn't appear to be losing interest.

I wasn't getting out until he left. Nor could I call anyone. My phone remained in my satchel outside the bin. Dumb and nothing to do about it now except hope he left soon.

Bang. Bang. The rhythmic pounding didn't stop and lulled me into a restless sleep.

When I woke suddenly, it took a moment to realize the pounding had stopped.

Had Ralph left?

I waited. Listened. Wondered if he stood just outside waiting for me to pop my head out so he could—

What I pictured next could be blamed on my best friend, Annie, who loved gory movies and guess who had to watch them with her?

A stirring to my left and a pair of glowing green eyes—slitted and no longer the pretty emerald-jewel version—showed a Goblin creeping from the bags. Or at least I hoped it was a Goblin. The rats in my town could be quite dangerous.

The lid of the dumpster creaked. I held my breath.

The goblin whistled as it turned its eyes in my direction.

"Is Ralph gone?" I asked.

Eyes bobbed up and down. Hopefully it meant yes.

Tense with fear, I rose and lifted the lid fully to look out upon the alley, dark still and yet lighter than the inside of the dumpster. I could see clear to the end of both sides of the alley. Ralph was gone.

Or so I thought until I swung a leg over the edge and looked down. A lump had settled on the ground.

Not a lump.

A body.

Missing its head.

The goblins squealed in joy as I puked my dinner all over the dumpster.

CHAPTER

THREE

A WITCH HAD ONLY TWO CHOICES WHEN CONFRONTED WITH A body. The first was to call the police and deal with suspicious detectives, who would automatically assume I was the reason why a body was missing its head. A few bad hags had given us good ones a bad reputation. It started when a Fire Witch turned a small town in Ontario into a literal hell hole. In her defense, it was mostly there already. Now it actually possessed a portal to the demon dimension to add to its charm.

Calling the cops would see me spending the night at the station. That would be the kindest scenario. Another would put me in a cell for a few days while a lawyer argued they had no evidence.

Neither appealed.

The other option? Deny, destroy, and pretend it never happened.

Ralph was dead. Nothing would change that. Me

going to jail would serve no purpose, especially since I didn't kill him.

Now you might wonder how little ol' me was supposed to take care of the body of a full-grown man. If I were a butcher shop...

Ahem. I don't do meat. Ever. I was a vegetarian, meaning, along with veggies and fruits, I only ate ethically sourced milk, cheese, and eggs. Before you ask how that's possible, my bestie, who happened to be a farmer, sold me the goods. Her animals—raised for personal consumption and selling to select others—produced more than she could ever use, and I was happy to take the surplus off her hands. It helped my little shop thrive among the eco-minded folk in my neighborhood.

As I eyed my satchel, and the phone I could almost see inside, I debated calling Annie. She owned a farm. Plenty of places to bury a body. However, did I really want to get her involved? Didn't seem like the thing a best friend would do. Although it should also be noted if I called, she'd show up with a shovel.

I could dig my own hole. If I were at home, my garden would help. Decaying bodies did make for good fertilizer. It was why some of the best flowers, especially asters, were found in graveyards.

How to get the body home, though? I'd walked to work. I couldn't exactly lug it down the sidewalk all the way to my place. It might cause some people to question.

I needed to borrow a car. From whom? Annie would insist on knowing why—and offer to help.

Feeling overwhelmed, I chose to ignore Ralph for a second and entered my shop. I needed a drink of juice to replenish myself and help my brain think.

I sipped wheat grass with a hint of calming lavender as I looked around to see what I had that might help. I kept a few plants in my shop but none big enough, even combined, to rid me of a body in the next hour. Not to mention I was loathe to contaminate them if the body didn't agree. Ralph might have been seriously ill.

I still remembered what happened to Mrs. McPherson's rose bush. Rumor had it the ornery old lady died of a heart attack while pruning it and landed in the prickly plant. The bush took care of the body, even mulched the bones, and turned into a raging, flesh-hungry beast with dripping blood-red flowers and poisonous petals. When the Cryptid Authority torched it, it was said all the plants in a mile radius wilted. The story was a sobering reminder you are what you eat.

By the time I finished my drink, I remained without a solution to my corpse problem. Meaning, only one option left. Two, actually: Annie or the cops? I pulled out my phone and grimaced at the screen as I pushed on the door to exit into the alley.

The choice of who to call got taken out of my hands. Why bother? The body was gone.

CHAPTER
FOUR

MAYBE I SHOULD HAVE SPENT MORE TIME SEARCHING FOR and questioning about the missing body; however, my day started at 5 a.m. Given the hour neared one, fatigue wasn't just tugging at me. It slammed my whole body.

Thank the goddess for taking care of my problem. No body. No blame.

I dragged my tired butt home, twitching at every movement. Whirling at every single benign sound. Despite seeing Ralph without his head, a part of me expected him to pop up.

Eyes barely open, I paid no mind to my house. I fell into my bed and managed a few hours of sleep. I woke at 4:50 a.m., on the dot, my body like a clock. I'd lost my ability to sleep in once I hit my thirties. Now peaking at forty—but happily passing for much younger—I truly was a morning person. I bounced out of bed and hopped in the shower—which I could get done efficiently in like three minutes, including brushing my teeth. By 4:57 I was out the door, a super caffeinated coffee in hand, skipping practically up the road. By 5:30, I had my first batch of muffins in the oven, my coffee drunk, and my next tray being readied for the ovens.

I started seeing people around sixish, as they needed their breakfast fix of muffins, scones, and wake-me up cappuccino pastries with a hex of extra wakefulness for those who struggled with the early hour. Once the morning rush ended, I prepped for the lunch crowd, the most in-demand item being the spelled double stuffed cookie that prevented falling asleep at the desk, some of my specialty cupcakes, and nut-filled pastries. Tarts, more cupcakes, and cream-filled puffs magicked with contentment rounded out my day's work for the afternoon and dinner crowd. It petered out at six usually, with me making it home by seven. Six days a week because I took Tuesdays off. Sundays, I started later.

Used to be I had an assistant to allow me more free time. Pietrov, a gangly boy training to be a witch, got accepted into the Academy of Magical Arts, and I'd yet to find a replacement. I missed him, especially since I knew I ran myself ragged; however, finding someone who could bake decently for what I could afford? Not easy. And that was without the ability to place hexes.

It made me wonder who had a son or daughter, like Pietrov, looking for an apprenticeship that paid. I might have to put out an ad before I collapsed from running myself ragged. I could also close earlier. Even an hour a day would do me some good.

The day passed quickly, but anxiously. During two lulls, I found myself at the door to the alley, peeking outside. No sign of the body, and despite dropping treats into the dumpster, the goblins remained hidden and quiet.

The busy afternoon cleared me out early, so by five, I flipped the sign in the door over and started doing my cleanup. A rattle at the entrance to the shop drew my gaze. I was ready to yell, "Closed," only to see Annie outside.

I'd completely forgotten delivery day. I unlocked and held open the door as Annie popped in with her dolly stacked with eggs, a few liters of milk and cream, plus some homemade cheeses.

Those who pictured a farmer would have never guessed Annie belonged to their ranks. My freckled friend enjoyed a mixed heritage that gave her tanned skin, almond-shaped eyes, full lips, and a wild, curly, ebony mane. Her plump frame strained at her T-shirt featuring today's vegetable—the eggplant—and I had to wonder at the pairing of skintight leggings with a Christmas pattern, especially considering Halloween was around the corner. Annie didn't care about fashion. She opted for comfort and pounced on huge discount sales— which often explained the holiday theme of her garments that could be bought for seventy percent off.

I locked the door behind her while she wheeled her dolly to the kitchen.

Once there, she whirled on me with wide eyes. "Have you heard?"

"Heard what?" I asked, trying to not wince as she slugged items onto the counter, the eggs tossed as casually as the milk.

"Apparently, everyone in the rehab has gone missing. You know, the one on Smythe Road. What's it called?" Annie tapped her chin.

"Second Chances. What do you mean everyone went missing? Have their guests escaped?" I called them guests for lack of a better word. If there'd been a breakout, it explained why Ralph had returned. It did not, however, excuse his sudden urge to bite me, eat those poor goblins, or diminish the fact he'd been decapitated and disappeared into thin air.

"Not just the people they had locked up, the staff, too. Every single one right down to the receptionist. Gone. Poof." She flung her hands in emphasis.

I arched a brow. "That's a lot of people. Where did they go?"

Annie shrugged. "No one knows. Rumor is the police were going to raid Second Chances, and so they scrammed."

"Why would the police be interested in the rehabilitation rehab?" Even weirder, why anyone would steal its patients.

"Someone complained about abuse and weird shit going on. Apparently sounded convincing enough they convinced the cops to pay it a visit, only once they arrived, they found the place empty but everything left behind. Clothes, plates, books, even cell phones and purses. As if everyone got up and walked away."

"That sounds impossible." Even if there'd been a fire evacuation or something of that sort, people would have grabbed their wallets and phones.

"Not impossible. I'm thinking there was an outbreak." Annie's expression lit up as she launched into her theory. "Something so contagious the government swooped in, dropped a sleeping bomb, and took everyone to a secret location."

Having been friends a while, I knew to expect crazy conspiracies from my best friend. Although, in this case, it wasn't necessarily a bad one. "You know, that makes sense. After all, it would take clout to coordinate the disappearance of that many people."

My acquiescence led to Annie skipping to her next —in her mind—plausible scenario. "Could also be aliens."

"Or some evil overlord kidnapping citizens of our town to create a super army to conquer the world." I threw out the most outrageous thing I could think of.

She nodded solemnly. "Let's hope not. But if it happens, you know where I keep the guns."

I did. Annie had several stashes because, unlike me, she was "make war, fuck love." She'd been burned in the past. Badly. I worried what would happen if the guy who hurt her ever dared show his face again.

"You can keep the guns. You know they freak me

out." I had other ways to defend myself. Better ways than Valerian root. Next time, I'd have a sprig of itchy sumac, maybe a length of rose thorn.

Being in tune with plants meant I knew what could cure and what could hurt. I also owned a few deadly gardening tools if I got desperate. The problem being the idea of doing harm turned my stomach.

Annie tsked. "You're too nice. It's good we're friends. You need me to protect you."

A bit insulting even if true. Look at how I handled Ralph. Thinking of whom, I really should tell her. "One of those missing folks ended up in the alley last night."

Annie's eyes widened. "Who? Was it Ralph?" She used to bring him romance paperbacks once she'd finished them. He'd read them and then light them for warmth. And before you ask, yes, I gave him a blanket. Several. And sleeping bags. He slept in them once then set them on fire.

Given how much Harry, the fire chief, had given me heck the last time he and the firemen from the Thirteenth Precinct came to put it out, I'd learned to avoid giving Ralph large flammable objects.

"It was Ralph, but there was something wrong with him. He tried to hurt me. I escaped but not before he bit a goblin in half." I wrinkled my nose.

"Ew." More fascination than actual disgust.

"Right?" I exclaimed. "I thought he was going to eat me, too, and I got all freaked out so I hid in the dumpster for like hours."

"You were attacked and didn't call me?" Annie asked, crossing her arms, miffed.

"I would have, only I dropped my phone when I climbed into the bin."

"Mindy! How many times does it have to be said? Never drop the phone." Annie punctuated the advice by slapping her hands.

"I know. Trust me, I wasn't happy given how long I had to hide with the garbage. It took forever before it was safe to come out."

"So where did Ralph go? Has he been caught? Because he sounds dangerous. Might have to rooster him."

She referenced Old Sal. The ornery cock got dropped off by someone who drove off too fast for Annie to ask questions. She took in the bird, who turned out to be a giant dick. He didn't just crow at dawn. It was always timed to be the most startling. Two a.m., followed by five minutes after she fell back asleep. While shaving her legs. Bringing a spoon of hot soup to her mouth. During sex.

Annie believed in treating animals with kindness —even those destined for her plate. Sal wasn't nice to her or any other creatures. Nor was his stringy ass edible, so she kicked him out. Put him outside the fence and told him to have a good life. It was a bad year for coyotes. Sal never was heard crowing again. On the one hand, Annie didn't actually have to kill him. She let nature take its course. But on the other...

don't get on her bad side. She would put you outside the fence.

I should have been shocked she'd even suggest doing it to a person, but this was Annie.

"Don't worry about Ralph. Someone already took care of him."

"Did the cops pick him up? Or the men in the white coats?"

"Neither. He got decapitated while I hid in the dumpster."

The statement dropped her jaw and silenced her. For like a millisecond. "What? A man lost his head and I'm only hearing about this now?" Annie shrieked.

Trust my friend to be mad she'd missed out on the action and not the actual crime. "I was too tired and in shock to call. Besides, I knew I'd see you tonight." A quick white lie.

She grimaced. "I missed all the fun."

"Hardly fun." My dry reply.

"Who killed him?"

"I don't know. I didn't see or hear anything. When I emerged, I found Ralph's headless corpse on the ground."

"Did you take a picture?" Her expression brightened.

I shook my head.

"Really, Mindy?" Peeved didn't begin to describe her tone. "No pic, no call."

"It was super late."

"You selfish cow. It's never too late to call your best friend for help."

"Sorry?" I kind of was in retrospect. At the same time, I didn't want to drag her into any muck. "Not sure what you could have done."

"So what did the cops say about the body?"

"They don't know because there is no body. While I was inside getting a drink, Ralph disappeared. I don't know where, or even how. I was only gone minutes."

"Meaning someone took it, or the body decomposed quickly. Did you see any sludge or ash in the area? Maybe smell something like brimstone?" While not a cryptid herself, Annie knew more about most species than I did. Despite my being consider a sub class of cryptid because of my magic, I barely passed my witch accreditation and never did learn to fly a broom, meaning I'd never achieve the rank of sorceress.

I shook my head. "I have no idea what happened other than Ralph was acting weird then he was dead and gone."

"Wait, do you think everyone that went missing is like Ralph and acting all kooky? What if they were contaminated with something? Could be the military followed him and cleaned up their mess."

"It's possible." I had only to recall Ralph's milky gaze and his bloodied mouth to admit there was something horrific at work.

"Do you think he infected you?" She narrowed her gaze on me.

Such a thing didn't occur until Annie mentioned it. Suddenly, my chest grew tight. "How would I know?" Earth magic had its limitations. Hexes and charms tied to an object could affect small changes. I could even directly channel power into people and things for a short time. But while I could ease ailments, my abilities didn't run to diagnosing them, especially in myself.

Annie held up her arm in front of my face. "Do you want a bite?"

"Ew. You know I don't like meat."

And neither did Ralph when he lived in the alley, which was when it hit me. The wrongness of his actions. The fact his headless body didn't leave any blood. No fluid at all. Surely someone being decapitated would create quite the mess.

"You just thought of something!" Annie jabbed a finger in my direction. "Spill it."

"What if Ralph somehow became a zombie? Which is nuts, I know. Zombies don't exist." Not in this day and age. The history books, though, did talk about how the last zombie attack, known as the Black Plague, almost wiped out humanity. After the necromancer animating the bodies died—decapitation being rather permanent—disease erupted because of the decaying bodies strewn across Europe. It led to the extermination of all necromancers, even the young, and a burning of their books.

"No zombies that we know of," my friend added.

"But never say never. Remember the unicorn they discovered last year?"

"Wasn't that debunked as a hoax?"

"Who can tell anymore? Between digital editing and the media covering up stuff for the government, we could be living in a necropolis for all we know."

That caused my lips to twitch. "I doubt the undead are eating my cupcakes."

"No, they're trying to eat you," Annie pointed out, squinting at me. "Are you sure he didn't bite you?"

"I'm fine." I rolled my eyes.

"For now." She hummed a few ominous notes. "What about the goblin he ate?"

"Less ate and more like bit it in two." The memory brought a shiver.

"Only one? Did he nick any of the others?"

I frowned. I didn't recall if he'd chomped any after the first. "I don't know. But I spent the night in the dumpster with a bunch of them. If one of them turned zombie, wouldn't I know?"

"If it was in there with you. Could be it took off, or it's hiding, biding its time." Annie didn't shy from the worst-case scenario.

"You're assuming a bite is all it takes." Just because movies and shows claimed becoming a zombie took only a small wound didn't make it true.

"Why don't we find out? Let's see your goblins." Annie marched to the back door and first eyed the ground—which lacked any blood or gooey stains—and then her gaze turned to the lip of the dumpster above her head. I pointed to a crate I kept there especially for putting out the garbage.

A hop on and she flipped back the lid. She poked her head in without hesitation as I exclaimed, "Careful."

Annie glanced at me. "Of what? There's nothing in here. It's empty."

CHAPTER
FIVE

What Annie claimed couldn't be true.

"The dumpster can't be empty. Garbage collection isn't for two more days." Yet a glance over the lip showed the bin cleaned out, and I mean clean as if pressure washed.

How was that even possible? I'd been out here a few hours ago, tossing out a full bag. I'd seen one of the goblins poking its green face from the pile. A pile now gone.

I should have heard something. Unless...

"Someone used magic." Most likely a noise dampening spell as they removed everything in the trash bin then an air scouring to remove all sediment. The question being, why?

Annie said it first. "I'll bet it's the government."

"More likely the Cryptid Authority." They were better equipped to handle things of a magical nature. Most governments had established agencies with specially trained staff to deal with the non-human because, after all, a rampaging minotaur in a china shop was a different beast to handle than a gun-toting villain in a bank.

"Either way, they're covering up something."

"Better hope not, because you do realize we are both involved."

"I'd like to see them try and make me disappear." Her scowl might have appeared fiercer without the dimple of excitement.

"I think the whole point is we wouldn't see them coming." Like the poor goblins. It seemed unlikely they'd been taken and kept alive.

"The mystery deepens," Annie declared, rubbing her hands in glee.

"Speaking of deep, you coming over for some deep dish pizza?" I asked as we headed back into my shop.

"That vegan shit you call pizza is an unholy abomination," she declared.

I protested. "It's got real cheese. Your cheese, I might add."

"Ruined by the green things on it."

"Vegetables are good for you."

"In moderation," she muttered. "A good thing I brought real food."

"You know I hate it when you cook meat." The smell and appearance bothered me.

"I know how you are about it, which is why I brought the fixings for my famous nachos."

"Now you're talking!"

We put away the groceries before locking up. As I checked the handle to ensure the door was secured, Annie muttered, "I'd swear it's watching me."

"What is?" I asked as I turned.

"The crow." She pointed to one sitting on a lamp-post. I wondered if it was the dive-bomber from the night before.

I kept an eye on it as we got into her truck. Despite it being within walking distance, Annie drove the few blocks to my place and parked at the curb. I owned a narrow townhouse that had a garden the width of my house in front instead of a driveway. Unlike my neighbors with their asphalt and stone walkways, I cultivated a jungle that did not cross any property lines. My plants knew better than to squat without permission.

As I stepped out, I breathed deep and smiled. Home.

I followed the narrow walkway comprised of paving stones, the moss spread over them a soft cushion for my feet. The tiger lilies, in their last late summer bloom, swayed on their stalks, and the flowers flexed in greeting. The railing of my porch held vines wrapped around that spread to the walls of my home and framed all the windows. The leaves shivered as I trailed my fingers over part of its stalk.

"Hello, Vinny." What my English ivy enjoyed being called. Older established plants formed identities that the perennial crops never managed.

I entered the house and Fern waved her fronds

frantically, my tropical vascular always happy. My prickly cactus, Fred, remained grumpy in the corner. As for Lois, my lavender plant, she emitted waves of calm.

Some people had cats or dogs, even rodents as pets. My home was filled with plants and the freshest air you could ask for.

Annie followed me inside grumbling. "Like walking into a haunted greenhouse."

Annie had issues with the way nature reacted around me. In her defense, she didn't have any magic, and while she might have a cryptid ancestor in her past, she showed no sign of it in the now.

"Plants are good for you and the planet."

"Not always true. Just last week in the news they had a story about some Venus fly trap that started eating people. They might not have caught it if the neighbors hadn't called the cops about some awful singing."

"It wasn't that bad." I'd seen the video. Heard the crooning. The Venus hummed up until the department of warrior botanists chopped its head off. Hard to feel too bad given the legs of a cop dangled from its mouth.

Annie snapped her fingers in front of me. "People over plants, remember? We had that talk."

"Never!" I stuck out my tongue. Although, in all honestly, I didn't want to see anyone hurt, plant, animal, human, or other.

"Throw on the news while I fix us up some

nachos." By news, she meant type our curiosity into a search bar and see what it spat out.

I searched for the obvious first: *missing people Second Chances rehab.* It didn't merit more than a few Tweets. None of the news stations had reported on it yet, which seemed odd. You'd think that many folks mysteriously disappearing would be worth a mention. Perhaps Annie's government conspiracy theory had some merit.

With the rehab being a dead end, I did a search on headless bodies. That returned some interesting results, none pertaining to my situation.

Annie emerged with a steaming platter of nachos. Homemade corn chips from corn sourced one hundred percent from her farm, hand milled, baked in her clay oven. Only one restaurant in town served them and charged a premium, they were that good. The salsa? Came from her garden, which I visited every few weeks to ensure its health. And of course, she used her own cheddar cheese, churned from cows exclusively free range.

"What did you find?" she asked, plopping beside me on the couch.

My kitchen table had been taken over by plants. I had a tendency of rescuing them from stores when they were about to die, nursing them back to health, and then giving them to people who could use some green in their life.

"I found squat," I admitted.

"Impossible. Give me that." She snared my tablet. "You're probably not looking for the right thing."

I munched on nachos as Annie typed *Zombies*. As you can imagine, that got a zillion useless—if fun—results.

She then did something complicated that narrowed down the references to those from our immediate area within the last few days. One page of results, only two links, both on social media.

The first had a shaky video of someone running while huffing. The description claimed it was the last known sighting of Penny Dunn.

"Didn't we know a Penny Dunn in high school?" I asked.

"Maybe. That was a long time ago." Annie wrinkled her nose.

I pointed to the screen. "It doesn't say who's supposed to be chasing her."

"Check the comments."

There were only three by a pair of people. One of them said, *Franko did it*. Followed by another user, *Franko's dead*. And the final gem, *He always did say he'd haunt her from the grave. #zombierevenge*

"That's not proof of anything," I argued.

"Fine. You want to dig deeper? Let's see who this Franko is."

While I ate nachos, Annie took us down an information rabbit hole.

Social media coughed up the fact Franko was

Penny's boyfriend and an addict. The whole family spoke of their happiness at him being chosen by Second Chances for rehab. Then the startling announcement Franco had died, a fact his mother found out by trying to visit. Her social media post ranted, *All I wanted was to see my baby boy. And they kept telling me no. But I wouldn't leave and finally they told me the truth. FRANKO IS DEAD.*

The video of Penny being chased came out two days later.

"I wonder if Franko turned out like Ralph." Which begged the question, what about Penny? We couldn't find anything on her, so we moved on to the next video that claimed zombies were active in our town.

The clip, again taken at night, appeared to show someone with an odd glaze to their eyes and a vacant expression on their face. The male wore trousers and an open white coat. In this case, the person filming held the camera and taped while shouting, "Back off, Tom. I don't want to hurt you, but I will if you come near me."

The threat did nothing to stop the freaky-eyed Tom from launching himself at the camera. The person filming hit the ground, and the camera jostled before it finished off facing upward, showing nothing, but we could hear the screams. And then, suddenly, a head went soaring past.

We both gasped.

"Did we just..." Annie mused aloud even as I rewound the video.

Sure enough, a head went flying over the phone. Tom's head, I should add. A minute later, someone big and thick, dressed in a long duster, wearing a bandanna over the lower half of their face and a wide-brimmed hat, stepped over the camera.

"Who was that?" Annie muttered, and yes, I zinged the video backwards for a second look.

"He reminds me of a gunslinger." Big and dangerous.

"Gunslingers don't slice off heads," was Annie's inane reply.

"Paladin. Knight. Doesn't matter." I glanced at my friend. "I think that might be the guy that took care of Ralph." Same *modus operandi*.

"Seems likely. We should find him."

"Find?" I ogled Annie. "Why would we do that?"

"Maybe he knows what's going on with those people."

I shook my head. "No. We should stay far away. He's obviously not the good guy. I mean, look at that." I pointed to the screen and the head halted midflight. "He's decapitating people."

"And? Who cares if they're zombies?" Annie rolled her eyes.

"We don't know that for sure. Could be they are ill. What if there's a cure?"

"Dead people can't come back to life," Annie reminded.

"Assuming they're dead."

"You're right. We should find out more."

While I wasn't keen about getting involved, the incident with Ralph kind of made it impossible to ignore. "Who do you suggest we ask?"

"Penny for starters." She pointed to the screen. "And whoever shot that video."

CHAPTER
SIX

PENNY PROVED EASY TO FIND. DEAD. ANIMAL ATTACK. THE news clip hadn't surfaced earlier because it lacked any mention of zombies.

"What shit reporting," Annie grumbled.

"In their defense, they did find her being chewed on by rats."

"Rats don't kill people." Annie didn't let Penny's demise change her mind. "Let's see if the other poster survived his attack."

Annie's plan to find the video-taker possessed a few flaws. For one, the person who uploaded the footage did so under a fake name. Sir-Wanks-a-lot-ola69 posted many clips, most of them odd furry-animal dress-up pics posing provocatively. Their face never showed in any videos, not even the zombie attack, which they'd posted with the caption: *It's finally happening.*

It might have seemed an odd statement, if I'd not

seen the "If you like this, watch this" videos in the sidebar. For some reason, the site had Sir-Wanks associated with end-of-the-world doomsday preppers. It made me think of Ralph. He'd believed it was coming.

After we demolished the nachos, and my pizza—which I garnished with pineapple from a can to please Annie—we had to admit defeat. No idea who posted the video, meaning we couldn't check and see if they were either A) a zombie, B) missing/vanished, C) fine, or D) playing a hoax online.

"Maybe we should stake out the morgue and see if Penny's body comes back to life," Annie suggested.

"Wouldn't she be at the funeral home?"

"Good thinking." Annie brightened. "Let's go check it out."

A plan dashed when the several funeral homes we contacted wouldn't tell us anything. The family hadn't yet posted viewing details, meaning we had no choice but to eat my moist vegan brownies.

It helped Annie's disappointment over coming up with only dead ends. She left but not before extracting a promise I would call her next time I encountered the possible undead or if I saw Mr. Long Duster.

Personally, I hoped neither happened.

Once she was gone, I went to bed, and before you freak, I will admit my choice was strange to most people.

As a kid, I'd had a waterbed, which I loved better than any mattress. However, it eventually broke, and given the trouble I got in when it flooded the apartment below at the time, my parents forced me to use a mattress. I hated it.

When I bought my townhouse, I went back to what I loved with a twist. My room held a hot tub, a big one, kept at a slightly elevated temperature, enough to keep the oversized lily pad I used as a bed from baking but warm for sleeping.

The flower, which Lilley had kindly grown off center, acted as a pillow. A second leaf covered me at night. I'd never slept better.

However, I'd learned to never show anyone other than Annie. The last guy I got serious with—meaning it lasted more than a few dates—took one look and ran out the front door. Apparently, a fear of drowning. He gave me an ultimatum, the bed or him.

Guess what I chose?

I went to bed hoping for sweet dreams. I woke to the rattle of tree limbs at my window. That would be Hugo, the tall pine from the yard next door. We'd become good friends since I prevented the neighbor from chopping him down—trees of a certain age enjoyed preservation status. The warning from Hugo's tapping branches had me slipping out of bed and searching for a robe.

As I went downstairs, I could see Vinny waving in agitation through the glass of my front door. I flung open the entrance and gaped. Entangled in Vinny's limbs were three vacant-eyed people in blue scrubs. But of more concern were the ones moving in the direction of my house from the sidewalk.

Not good. I slammed the door and locked it. Thick wood, it should hold. A peek to my side showed the beautiful, single-pane bay window. It wouldn't take much to shatter it.

Maybe I should leave. I headed for the back sliding door to my tiny patio, only to pause at the moving shadows outside. Several more of the freaky people approached, undeterred by the plants that sought to grab at limbs.

Were they zombies? Depending on the movie, they could open doors or climb stairs. I really hoped this was the dumb kind as I trotted back up to the second floor. As I hit the landing, I heard the tinkling of breaking glass.

Uh-oh. A glance around showed not much to barricade the stairs with. I entered my room and shut the door. No lock since I lived alone. I usually never even closed the door. My bedroom didn't offer much in way of protection.

Hence why my gaze went to the window. Hugo's branches scratched. While not ideal, I could climb him. A quick look down showed a swarm of bodies on the back porch. Moving to the front bedroom, over-looking the front yard, I noticed the zombies entangled in Vinny, while a few others clustered at the window they'd shattered. If they got inside, then I'd be better off out.

I shoved the window open and then hesitated. I should get some clothes on first rather than wander around in my robe. It took me only a minute to dress, a minute that had me cursing because all my shoes were downstairs, along with my wallet and phone. Oh, coconuts.

Thump. Thump. The noise indicated these zombies could climb stairs and had some kind of hunting ability since they immediately began pounding on the spare bedroom door, but it was the turn of the knob that had me sitting on the windowsill, legs dangling.

Vinny stilled his rustling branches, and I eyed the drain spout. Not ideal for climbing, yet my options remained limited. I grabbed hold and swung my body out. The ominous creak had me clinging to the wall, toes digging through the gaps between Vinny's limbs into the brick underneath. Technically, I was only about a dozen or so feet above ground. Not a devastating jump unless I broke something and couldn't run. If that happened, I'd be a zombie snack for sure.

Better descend a bit before attempting to leap. I concentrated on my grip as I inched down, so focused that when a slimy set of fingers grabbed hold of my ankle, I uttered a piercing shriek and kicked.

Surprisingly, my foot connected. I jerked free and reversed direction, climbing up instead of down, wanting to get out of reach.

Only when I'd reached the second floor once more did I dare a peek down. I cringed as the zombie who'd grabbed me, their unhinged jaw hanging lopsided, stood below, hand in the air, grasping. Of more concern, the zombies converged below, attempting to bust into my house.

Dagnabbit. Now what? I appeared stuck.

Which was when *he* appeared.

The man in the long leather duster stepped onto the curb, mighty sword in hand. The blade of it gleamed as he swung. One head flew over the holly bush. Another over the bonsai I'd been playing with. The third and fourth were caught by my tiger lilies.

After that I stopped paying attention because I'd heard an ominous creak. Vinny rustled in warning.

"I am not fat," I muttered as I did my best to disperse my weight. *Ping.* A screw loosened on a bracket.

The agitation of my ivy increased.

"I know. I know. I need to get down. Give me a second." I peeked down to see if my path was clear. Leather Duster stood below me, sword tip down in the dirt. More worrisome, he appeared to be waiting for me.

Maybe I should return to the spare bedroom and hope for the best.

Crack! The gutter broke.

As I fell, my head hysterically sang, *And down will come Mindy, drainpipe and all.*

CHAPTER
SEVEN

I HALF EXPECTED TO HIT THE GROUND. WOULD I LOSE MY head or a limb to the freaky dude in the gunslinger's coat? Despite holding a sword in one hand, he caught me! One armed, I should add, and he didn't even stagger.

Showoff.

I cracked open one eye and croaked, "Am I alive?"

"You tell me," he drawled.

"Do dead people piss themselves?" Because I came pretty damned close.

"You're not dead." He set me on my feet. The arm he'd managed to wrap around me was thick like the rest of him.

"Well, that's good to know," I quipped, taking a step away to stare into a partially masked face that revealed nothing but the clearest blue eyes I'd ever seen. "Who are you?"

"No one." He glanced away from me to the front door. "Are there more in the house?"

"No idea. I left when they decided they were coming in. They infested the backyard, too."

Without a word or semblance of asking permission, he entered my home. Vinny didn't try to block his path but rather kept his vines tight to the trellis. Given the sharp sword Mr. Catch-Me-One-Armed carried? Probably smart thinking.

I hugged myself as I glanced around. There were five headless corpses in my front yard and spilling into the neighbor's. Good news, no blood. The bad...

How would I explain this to the police? I had no doubt someone had called, probably even recorded the fight, and now I stood amidst the carnage. The proof of my fear came in the sudden eruption of sirens in the distance. Wouldn't be long before I was trying to explain how all these people came to be headless on my lawn.

Then again, it wasn't me who wielded the sword. As if thinking conjured Mr. Let-Me-at-Them, he emerged from my house. He stalked toward me, coat flaring, giving off a strong gunslinger vibe, but the sword in his hand made him more of a bad-boy knight.

Given the expression on his face, I half expected him to keep on walking past, but he halted and frowned at me.

When he said nothing, I fidgeted and mumbled, "Did you find any, uh, *things*?" Calling them zombies with Annie was one thing, but with this stranger, I hesitated.

"Too many. Who are you?" he asked.

"Mindy and you are?" I held out my hand.

"No one. Why did they come for you?"

"Because I make the best cupcakes in town?"

"They don't eat."

"Then I have no idea." I shrugged.

"There must be a reason." His head turned as the sirens grew decidedly louder. Without another word, he strode toward the road.

"Where are you going?"

"Away."

"And leaving me with this mess? I don't think so. The police are going to want to talk to you."

"Not interested." He kept walking.

I darted to stand in front of him and waved a hand at my front yard. "You can't take off. How am I supposed to explain all these decapitated bodies?"

"You won't." His non-reply as he strode past me.

I might have chased him down, only lights came on in the neighbor's house. What was I going to do? How could I keep myself from getting arrested?

Mr. Leroy emerged in a bathrobe and slippers, his gray hair standing in spikes. He shook a finger. "Evil witch."

At least once a week he harangued me about my service as a witch to Mother Earth. Made no bones about the fact he wanted me to move. Unfortunately for him, I liked my place. I'm sure he'd been giddy when he saw the commotion at my place. Probably thought he could finally rid himself of me.

Not today he wouldn't.

"Hello, Mr. Leroy." I waved and smiled.

I got a scowl in reply. "Your friend. He murders. I saw him."

"Yeah. So about that..." As I struggled for an excuse, my gaze fell to the ground and the empty moss. No body lay upon it. Had it risen and walked away? Without a head, that seemed unlikely.

It occurred to me, as I looked around, that there wasn't a single corpse left. Nor any craniums.

Well hot fudge on a caramel sundae. That was excellent news. Even as I had no idea what it meant.

I turned a bright smile on Mr. Leroy. "That wasn't real, Mr. Leroy. It was an, um"—my mind whirred and came up with an epic reply—"a hologram. My friend's been working on it. Imagine if virtual reality didn't require a headset and everyone could participate." It sounded entirely plausible, enough so that Mr. Leroy came down off his steps to poke at the grass and walkway with his cane.

"I saw it. He cut off their heads!" He waved the cane in my direction as the police arrived in their cruisers.

They piled out with guns, shouting, "Put down your weapon."

I put my hands up and waited.

Mr. Leroy kept shaking his cane. "She's a witch. Arrest her."

Never mind the fact being a witch hadn't been a crime in hundreds of years. Some humans still couldn't handle our existence.

"Put down the weapon!" Another shout.

I sighed. "It's okay, officers. He's harmless." Though since his wife died of cancer, a little bit addled. It helped me be more compassionate.

One officer lowered his weapon to approach, tilting his head as he said, "Ma'am, we got a report of a disturbance. Something about a man with a sword beheading people." His expression remained level, but his voice held a lilt of incredulity.

"As I was just telling Mr. Leroy, my friend was testing some new gaming equipment. Super realistic. Think the holodeck in *Star Trek*."

"Not fake. The body was here!" Mr. Leroy jabbed his cane at the ground.

Both cops holstered their weapon as the second one muttered, "What is wrong with people tonight? This is the second call we've had about dead bodies disappearing."

The first police officer noticed my broken window, which would cost me a pretty penny to fix. "What happened?"

I lied some more. "My friend needs to tweak his game a bit. He miscalculated and smacked into it."

"So, what's the name of the company he works for?" the second cop asked nonchalantly.

"Can't say. Wouldn't want to be accused of insider trading." I pretended to zip my lips.

The implication led to both of the officers suddenly realizing they had to be elsewhere. Mr. Leroy harangued them to the car, hoping they'd charge me with something.

As for me, I kept a fake smile pasted to my lips as I waved goodbye to them and my less-than-neighborly neighbor.

I reentered my house, closed the door, leaned against it, and sighed. Finally, I could digest what happened. Only it had happened so fast I'd not had a chance to really process.

The people who attacked my house wanted to hurt me. Mr. Leather Coat came to the rescue, bearing a sword like a knight of old. I lived, shaken, confused, and in need of calming.

Tea. A nice warm, soothing tea would be just the thing for my nerves. I entered my kitchen, only to freeze at a noise. I whirled to see a zombie coming at me from the dining room.

I didn't think, I acted, flinging my hands in the direction of my massive hanging spider plant, Peter, with its many tendrils.

Help. I pushed magic and thought at the greenery, and it replied, its long, dangling stalks writhing. They extended as they reached to grab the shambling, clearly ill woman. The tendrils wound around her, pinning her arms to her body.

Still, she aimed for me, sightless, yet somehow sensing my presence. A plant limb around her neck squeezed tighter and tighter. The woman with milky white eyes and snapping teeth did nothing to remove the plant. Her legs struggled to walk, but Peter had a firm grip.

I neared enough to look into her eyes, the sightless orbs not registering me. Her teeth clacked just like Ralph's had. The biggest difference being how much she stank. As if she'd rolled in something dead.

Because she is *dead.* Never mind the fact dead things didn't walk. The more I looked at her, the more I sensed the wrongness. The decay. The lack of life despite all twitching evidence.

I might be compassionate, but I wasn't stupid. I couldn't release her, and I doubted what ailed her could be fixed. The right thing didn't mean I could watch as my plant kept squeezing, the vine acting as garrote that first choked—not that she seemed to breathe—and then collapsed her throat before finally severing the head from the body.

Thud.

I turned around and put a hand to my stomach at the sight of the head lying face up, the jaw still moving as if it were capable of eating. So gross and not what I wanted to be watching; however, I forced myself to stare. The bodies outside disappeared quickly. Would this one do the same? I did a silent count in my head. *One Mississippi, two...*

At two hundred and three, the body deflated as if someone let out all the air. Then it dehydrated rapidly, everything getting dryer and tighter, even the clothes, until it got so insubstantial as to be—

Gone.

Spontaneous eradication. A theory I'd only ever heard of in college. It wasn't supposed to be possible, but then again, neither were zombies. Journals theorized that both, zombies and spontaneous eradication, could be done, but the knowledge had been lost intentionally. Some magic should never be practiced.

Tell that to whoever was making zombies and then ensuring no evidence remained to prove it.

Seriously, like what was their problem with me? Three a.m. and no way I'd go back to sleep. I gathered my things, including an overnight bag, and called a taxi to take me to my shop. I'd sleep on the tiny cot I'd bought years ago when getting my place fumigated for spiders. Sleeping at Annie's wasn't an option, not if someone was sending the walking dead after me.

Which begged the question, why? If they didn't like witches, then I hardly counted. My little hexes weren't all that powerful. Or did this have to do with Ralph? Did they want to eliminate me because I'd seen him or because they thought I'd killed him?

It wasn't as if I could tell anyone the truth. Or even ask what happened. I had no idea who the sword-slinger was. He'd come to my rescue and then left. Would I see him again?

I had no way of knowing. What did become clear? My town had a serious problem.

It didn't improve overnight. I slept in my shop, doors locked tight, pans layered across doorways as added noise protection. My anxiety woke me often and early.

Being unable to sleep left me browsing the news, which was how I caught the surge of people checking into the hospital after getting bitten. And not just bitten, in some cases missing flesh, as if gnawed on. The victims claimed a person did it, which, of course, led to claims of zombies, only there weren't any bodies to prove that theory, and none of those bitten turned into cannibals. The news called it mass hysteria caused by something environmental. They recommended boiling water.

Dumb. They should have encouraged people to invest in machetes.

That afternoon, Annie made sure I had something to defend myself with. She popped by with a scythe used at harvest. She relayed how she heard from a friend whose cousin knew a guy that claimed the biting thing was related to the missing folks from Second Chances. According to this same guy, no one should worry; the government was in the process of rounding them up to treat them for the illness caused by a chemical spill.

"What spill?" I'd asked.

"The one that starts us on a route to becoming mutants," was Annie's excited reply.

That didn't make me feel better, especially since everyone coming into the shop was talking about it. They had no idea what we were dealing with. Technically, I didn't either, but I did know of someone who did.

Where had Mr. Catch-Me-One-Handed gone? If only I had a way to find him. I had questions.

The next day he appeared in my kitchen.

EIGHT

I DIDN'T EXPECT TO SEE MR. MYSTERIOUS IN MY SHOP. I swung the empty tray in my hands before I could think twice.

Boing. I hit him in the head.

Oops.

The man in the leather duster appeared less than impressed.

As for me? I was very upset I'd ruined my favorite tray. It now had a massive dent in it. "Dang it." I rubbed the spot.

"I'm fine," he said dryly.

His bandanna remained around his neck, meaning I got to see his square-jawed and shockingly handsome face. Usually murderers only allowed that if they planned to leave no witnesses.

Despite that, I had a glare and a tart reply. "If you don't want to get bonked, don't startle people by being in places you shouldn't. How did you get in here?"

"Alley door."

"It's locked." A woman who worked by herself didn't leave doors unlocked even in the daytime.

Rather than explain how he got in, he said, "I didn't want to be seen coming in through the front."

I backed away. I could think of one disturbing reason he didn't want to be noticed. "Are you here to kill me like you did those people?"

He snorted. "I didn't kill anyone. The undead stop being people the moment they rise again."

"So those were definitely zombies." Nice to have confirmation.

"In the flesh, so to speak."

"Do you have to take their heads to get rid of them?" I asked.

"No. You can also set them off fire, squash them flat, or stake them out until they decompose." My mouth rounded in horror as he finished with a casual, "Catastrophic damage to the body breaks the animation."

"Animated like puppets?"

"Enough of the questions." He slashed a hand through the air. "I want to know why they came after you."

"You tell me. How did you know they'd be at my house?" Because no denying he'd been there on purpose.

"Purely accidental. I came across their scent and tracked them."

His use of "scent" had me asking, "Are you a werewolf?"

While not many admitted to it, their existence had been documented. Turned out, Lycanthropy—as they called the syndrome—like magic, was a genetic thing. Either you were born with it or not. In the Lycanthropy cases, it tended to be a recessive gene and could go generations without showing, so those who inherited the whole furry full-moon syndrome often found themselves surprised the first time it happened. Back in the day, a good number of werewolves were shot before Lycanthropy was classified as a disease. Now, if the authorities suspected rampaging werewolf on a full moon, they called in the specialists with their tranq guns. Once a werewolf was identified, they were court mandated to sign themselves into the closest police station for voluntary overnight lock up during full moons.

"Not a wolf." He denied it, and yet my tiny witchy sense could tell he wasn't all human. A lot of cryptid flowed through his veins. I just couldn't pinpoint what exactly.

"Nor are you a warlock." I cocked my head as I eyed him. "Part giant?

"No."

Getting words out of him proved harder than icing a cake with exactly one thousand and three rosettes, because the bride claimed it was lucky. "Incubus." Because he was damned sexy without that mask today. He'd tugged it down around his neck, so I got the full effect of his square jaw, rugged features, and those crystal-blue eyes.

His lip almost curved. "Definitely not."

"You're not human," I stated boldly.

"Yup." Apparently that was all I was getting.

Until I knew more, I'd be careful of him. "Thanks for saving me." I placed my bent tray to the side. Maybe I'd take a mallet to it and see if it could be salvaged.

"Didn't do it to save you." He didn't appear comfortable with my thanks.

"Pretty sure you're still a hero."

"Fuck no." The idea repugned him.

"Can I ask how you came to be hunting zombies? Where are they coming from? Did we have some kind of outbreak?" I peppered him with questions, and his grimace deepened with each one.

"You're supposed to be answering my queries."

"I will once you tell me more."

He scowled at me.

"Don't give me that look. You cut off some heads without a word of explanation then disappeared, only to reappear by breaking into my shop. Of the two of us, I think I deserve to know what in tarnation is going on."

"Tarnation?"

"Too strong?" I sucked in my lower lip. "Sorry. I should have gone with heck."

His brows rose. "Are you for real?"

Being impulsive I grabbed his hand and put it on my chest. "You tell me."

For a second, his lips parted, his gaze met mine, and something electric flowed between us. Then he jumped back as if I'd jabbed him with Mr. Leroy's cane.

"The zombies are the work of a necromancer I've been following."

Aha, apparently all I had to do for answers was invade his space and make him uncomfortable. Pity his first answer was a complete fabrication. "Necromancers don't exist." Given their tendency for evil, they'd been hunted to extinction. Rasputin had been the last known one.

Mr. Tall and Mysterious shook his head. "Guess again."

"You want me to believe we have a necromancer in town raising the dead." My lips pursed.

"You saw the zombies."

"I saw animated corpses, yes, but that doesn't mean it's a necromancer. Rumor is the government is covering up a chemical spill."

The scoffing expression had me almost cringing. "I thought you more intelligent than that."

"How would you know if I was smart? We've barely met."

"I've been watching you," he admitted, and I could tell he wanted to take it back.

"Spying?" I glanced down at my body. "If I'd known, I would have put on something a little sexier at night and given you a good show." My smile was pure mischief, and I swear his cheeks turned ruddy as he cleared his throat.

"Not that kind of watching," he grumbled.

"Why not?" I asked, taking too much pleasure in his discomfiture.

"Can we get back to the zombies?"

"Sure. Because I really want to know why they're suddenly popping up all over."

"A necromancer raises zombies for one reason only."

"And what reason is that?"

He arched a brow. "World domination."

That made me laugh. "Who the heck is striving for world domination in our little town?" Population less than twenty-five thousand. We didn't boast any major energy industry or resource unless the local tech company, Crypto-Backo, counted. We couldn't be more mundane if we tried.

"Every attempt to take over the world starts small."

"And has failed," I pointed out. "The closest we came to being under one supreme leader was when that mega-billionaire Muscksey bought up all the telecom companies in secret and shut down the internet, only to relaunch it as a propaganda outlet projecting his beliefs and agenda. His cyber reign of terror ended when he slipped and fell off his toilet." I didn't mention the part about his malfunctioning bidet. Rumor had it an assassin with magical ability hexed his fancy butt throne.

Mr. Leather Duster seemed unimpressed at my knowledge of history. "Are you being deliberately obtuse, or did I catch you on a good day?"

I grinned. "Just making conversation."

"I'm being serious."

"Come on. You're talking about the middle of nowhere. Why would a necromancer bother? What if you're wrong and it is a chemical spill or swamp gas?"

"Which is more plausible?"

Honestly, at this point, I couldn't have said. The whole situation proved way out there. "I'm thinking Annie might be right. It's aliens."

Rather than reply, he eyed me and the kitchen we stood in. "You've been doing magic in here." Stated, not asked.

"I have, and, yes, I am certified. My license to practice is out front."

He grunted. "What kind of magic?"

"I am a daughter of the Earth." As opposed to the old school Wiccan or the modern Kinetic kind, I served Mother Earth, the one true goddess.

"You spell the food you sell?"

"Not all of it." Offering too much of something made it lose value. By convincing people of the effort involved and constricting the number for sale at any given time, it added to the price and prestige. "I offer a few basic hexes baked into certain treats."

"Are you capable of learning a new spell?"

"Are you capable of not being rude?" I asked tartly, only to immediately exclaim, "Silly me, apparently you aren't."

"I meant no offense. I want to ensure I didn't waste my time."

"Your time?" I arched a brow. "What about wasting mine?"

Rather than reply, he kept on his tangent. "I take it you have everything you need to cast a spell?"

"Why does it matter?"

"Because I am going teach you a hex to repel the dead."

I blinked. "Wait, what?"

"Me. Teach. You. Hex. Repel. Zombies." He repeated his statement slowly as if I were stupid, and I must be because it made no sense.

"Does such a thing even exist? And if it does, how do you know it?" Because I could tell he lacked magic. At least the kind familiar to me.

"Does it matter how I know?"

"Yes, it does. How do I know what you're teaching me is one"—I held a up a finger—"an actual spell, two, it does what you say, and three, that it's safe? Hexes can be dangerous if improperly cast." I once knew a girl who tried to improve her eyesight but got sloppy and instead combined her orbs into a large one. In good news, the last lonely cyclops in the world got to continue his family name.

"Do you want to learn it or not? Because I have better things to do than argue with you." He narrowed his gaze on me, but I didn't back down. Not with my safety at stake.

"You know, it would be a lot more confidence inspiring if you just answered a few questions rather than being Mr. I'm-So-Tough-and-Mysterious. I don't even know your name."

"Because it is not important."

"And yet you expect me to learn magic from you. A perfect stranger who won't give me even the most basic info."

"I'm not showing you magic, just the shape of a hex."

"A hex that will use magic to do something. Same thing."

"Not really," he argued.

"You and I really aren't starting off right, so let's have a do-over. Hi, I'm Mindy." I held out my hand.

He glared rather than shake it.

Undaunted, I smiled and waggled my fingers. "Your turn. My name is..."

"Reiver. Fuck. Are you done playing around?"

"Where are you from, Reiver?"

"Do you want to learn the hex or not?"

I did, and the more I antagonized him without him actually snapping and killing me, the more confident I became. "You swear it actually does what you claim and won't cause me or others harm?"

He put a hand to his chest. "I swear."

The vow, the fact he meant it, hit me in a shiver.

"Well, then, yes, teach me. And tell me more. You said it repels the zombies."

"In a sense. It renders people invisible to their senses, making them less likely to be harmed."

"Diverting their attention. Which leads to question two, do zombies crave flesh?"

"Yes."

"Do they need it to survive?"

"No, because they're dead and the animation doesn't stop the decay from happening. Hence why necromancers constantly need a fresh supply of bodies."

"Seems like a rather inefficient army. Couldn't you defeat the necromancer simply by waiting him out and ensuring no access to fresh bodies?" Which reminded me, I should really get a will done demanding I be incinerated. My ashes would be quickly absorbed by Mother Earth.

"It's not just humans he can animate. Anything dead is his to play with."

For some reason I thought of an army of bugs and shuddered. "So how do we repel the dead? How long does the hex last? Does it require any special ingredients?"

"My understanding is pumpkin and cinnamon are best for enhancing the protection."

"The flavors of Halloween, quelle surprise," I mocked.

"Did you think those came about by accident?" he sneered.

I opened my mouth for a snarky reply just as the bell of my shop dinged. "One second." I hated running out, but I quickly took care of the client and then flipped the sign to say "Back in an hour." As I did, a glance out showed a crow on the sidewalk. A sleek-looking specimen that cocked its head at me and opened its beak.

Probably the same jerk that attacked me in the alley. Interesting that it usually appeared when zombies did. Connected or just a carrion bird following its next meal?

I half expected Reiver to be gone before I made it back to the kitchen, but he stood there, coat shed and hung on a hook by the back door, looking incongruous beside my pink rain slicker and purse. He wore a black T-shirt, tight to his broad chest, bulging over his biceps. His matching dark jeans molded his thick thighs. I saw no sign of his sword. Maybe he only carried it at night.

"Have you eaten?" I asked, heading for the fridge and the lunch I'd ordered from the sandwich place next door. I'd bought an oversized sub to split for lunch and dinner.

"The spell?" he growled.

"Yes, yes, we'll get to it, but while we discuss it, we should eat. I hate doing magic on an empty belly."

He sighed but didn't argue. He eyed the sandwich I placed in front of him, along with the bag of chips I'd opened.

In between bites, I asked my questions. "How long does the spell last?"

"Depends on the amount of magic infusing the hex. A few hours at least. Ingested gives the best results."

A common thing with spells. A token only radiated a certain distance, meaning a person required overlapping hexes for full coverage when it came to defense, for example. But digesting a hex spread the spell throughout a body for an all-over effect. On the negative, it tended to disappear more quickly as the body burned through it.

"Where did you learn the spell?" I asked after a swallow of my matcha green tea.

"I came across it in my travels."

"And how do you know it does what you say it does?"

"This isn't my first run-in with the undead."

"Oh," I muttered. "So you're a zombie hunter then."

"Of sorts."

"And you do this to make the world a better place."

He snorted. "No."

"Then why?"

At my repeated questions, he sighed. "Why does it matter?"

When I just stared, he gave in.

"I was hired by the Cryptid Authority."

My brows almost shot off my face in surprise. "They know about the zombies?"

"They do now. I was brought in to see if their suspicions were true. And then asked to handle it."

"How come no one's heard about the problem?"

That brought a low chuckle. "Because telling the populace the walking dead are an issue seems like a bad idea."

My brow creased. He might have a point. "If you're working legit for the CA, then why the cloak-and-dagger routine?"

"I see no need to advertise my presence. My role is to handle things discreetly."

"I wouldn't call cutting off heads in my front yard discreet."

"What heads?" he asked with a slow smile.

"Do you know what happens to the body? Why they disappear"

"It's the animation effect. It requires much negative magic, which is contained so long as the body is more or less intact. Once it starts to seep, the rebalancing of the forces eliminates the negative source, resulting in the esoteric combustion of the remaining structure."

I blinked at the mouthful of mumbo jumbo. "In other words, dead zombies disappear. Got it." As I pulled out ingredients to bake some pumpkin spice cupcakes with a vanilla buttercream frosting, I found myself with more questions. "The other night, was that you who took care of Ralph in the alley?"

He nodded. "I came across his trail and followed it."

"If you can do that, why haven't you backtracked to find where they're coming from?"

"I tried. I originally went to the rehab where the Cryptid Authority received its first report of strangeness. By the time I came on the scene, the place was cleared out. From there, I isolated the tracks of that male the other night in the alley behind your store and handled it."

"What about the zombies at my house?"

"Dropped off in front of your house by a van. No license plate or markings."

Only one way he could have known that. "I still can't believe you were spying on me!"

"A good thing wouldn't you say?"

If he'd not arrived, I might have been zombie lunch. "Why?"

"Because."

"That's not an answer."

"Call it a hunch then. One that paid off."

The implication hit me. "Them being dumped outside my place indicates someone's targeting me."

"Yes."

"Why?" Who on Earth had I annoyed that badly?

He shrugged. "You tell me."

"I have no enemies." My job was bringing sweet, sugary joy to the world and making it a cleaner, better place.

"You are a witch."

"Yes, but by no means powerful." I didn't have many other Earth witches to compare myself to;

however, if the history books could be believed, those who truly were close to the goddess could literally do environmental miracles. Grow not just a tree from a seed in days but an entire forest. Me? My specialty was healthy house plants and baking.

"The reason soon won't matter because if you ever stop talking, I'll teach you how to repel future attacks. Keep in mind this hex will protect your person if ingested but can also be used on doorways and windows for added defense. Although, be warned, the spell only works to prevent zombies from seeing. They can still harm."

"Meaning don't bump into them."

"Exactly."

As I began making the batter for the cupcakes I'd be using for the spell, I asked, "How many should I bake?"

"As many as you can. If I don't find the necromancer soon, they'll be needed to stop the coming wave of zombie attacks."

CHAPTER
NINE

"Are you expecting an army of zombies to hit my town?" I asked as I tripled my batch of ingredients while also picking my jaw up off the floor.

"Yes."

"But where is the necromancer getting the bodies? You said they need them fresh. I doubt enough people in this town are dying every day to supply them."

"Which is why he'll take who and what he needs. The emptying of the rehab is an example of his ruthlessness."

"You keep saying he."

"Necromancers are always male."

My feminism reared its head. "Not always. Wasn't Nefertiti one?"

"She died too long ago to be sure. And again, even if she were, no other female necromancers have been encountered since."

"Hunh. That's kind of sexist," I mumbled as I

poured batter into the cupcake tins. I popped the three trays, twenty-four cupcakes each, into the oven, and then I leaned on it, enjoying the radiating heat. "Those will take twenty minutes. While I mix up the icing, tell me more about yourself."

"No."

I turned my back so he couldn't see my smirk of amusement. "Why not?"

"Because."

"My mother used to say because is not an answer."

"I'm not here for social games." His reply was disgruntled.

"No, just asking me to trust you. Expecting me to employ an unknown hex and actually give it to people. Because that sounds like such a sane thing to do, given we met, like what, five minutes ago."

"Days."

"I would hardly think that counts, given during the first encounter I never saw you and the second time you ran off without an explanation. And now you show up and expect me to believe every word that comes out of your mouth. How do I know you are who you say you are?"

He stared at me for a second. "Fine. If it will set your mind at ease, what do you want to know?"

"Are you single?"

He flattened his lips. "How is this relevant?"

"I'm trying to gauge what kind of guy you are. By the way, I am single and into men." I threw that out there. Always good to make a status known in these times. It avoided complication and confusion later.

"What makes you think I care?"

"More like you probably already guessed if you've been watching me for days. Seems only fair since you've got a head start on me that you divulge a bit about you. You know, in the spirit of open and honest communication." I skirted around him, maybe closer than necessary, to hit the fridge for butter to make the frosting.

A heavy sigh preceded his mumbled, "I'm single, but I don't have time to date."

"Who said anything about dating?" I tossed a wink over my shoulder. Now that I'd gotten over my initial disquiet, I had to admit the big guy got my petals fluttering. Usually, I didn't go for the burly, gruff type, but something about Reiver had me a little more outspoken than usual.

Talk became almost impossible, as my mixer emitted a ton of noise. While it ran, he popped into the front of my shop and returned looking grim. He then ducked his head out the back door.

Once I stopped the mixer, I asked, "What's got your face looking as if you've been sucking lemons?"

"Your building is being watched."

"By who? Where?"

"Not who, what. I can't tell what the creature is other than it is dead."

My nose wrinkled. "That doesn't sound good."

"Don't worry. I'm here." Two simple statements

and yet they inspired more confidence than I understood. It helped he proved blasé and knowledgeable
about the zombies, even matter of fact about how to
handle them.

"What about when you leave?"

"You'll know how to hex yourself for protection."

"What if the necromancer sends someone who
isn't dead yet? I mean you gotta figure he's got some
living lackeys. How else would he get groceries and
stuff?"

"Guess you'd better be careful."

"Easily said when you're six-two, probably about
two hundred plus pounds to my five-four, a hundred
and forty."

Reiver frowned. "You're a witch. You can protect
yourself."

"I don't know what kind of witches you usually
hang with, but I'm the kind who does no harm." After
what I'd recently done, I amended, "To living things."

"Defending yourself isn't causing harm."

"Obviously, but I'm pointing out that some of us
are better equipped than others."

"Buy a weapon."

"I have one and I'd rather not even have to think of
using it," I grumbled. "I'd like for this necromancer to
not involve me in whatever plot he has going. What
have I done to deserve it?"

"I'm thinking it might have to do with the undead
I handled in your alley the other night. It could be they
think you're a threat."

My eyes widened. "The necromancer thinks I'm a zombie killer?"

"Possibly."

"But I'm not!" I exclaimed. "You are!" On the outside, technically it might appear as if it were me. After all, the zombie ambush at my house also ended up in carnage. I sat down heavily on a stool. "How do I fix this?"

"You can't. I need to find this necromancer and stop them." A grim declaration that had me eyeing him.

"And how do you propose doing that?"

"The necromancer will make a mistake at one point, and when they do..."

"You'll kill them."

"Yes." He didn't even pretend otherwise.

Let him. Not my fight. With the icing ready, I threw some in a piping bag and held it over a plain wafer that would act as my canvas. "Show me this hex."

CHAPTER

TEN

The hex to repel zombies proved to be simple in design. I recognized the teardrop shield aspect as the part that provided protection, the oval around that a mirror to reflect. A trio of symbols all relating to life and living things added some more complicated flair.

Once I finished drawing it, I inspected it with a critical eye. All the shapes that needed closing showed no gaps. The symbols nested within each other. A pretty design that would do nothing until I added the magic.

For small things, say like a single hex, I could draw upon my internal reservoir. As a daughter of the Earth, I carried some of her magic with me. I replenished by communing with my goddess—meaning I connected often with dirt. Mud being my favorite. It left my skin so soft. Another reason my neighbor hated me; every time it rained, I was outside jumping in the muddiest puddles.

I held my hand over the drawing and pushed my magic in its direction, causing it to glow a light green that hued on yellow before finishing in silver. The aura of magic faded, and I squinted at my drawing. The hex appeared to be active.

I poked at it with the tip of my finger, smearing the markings onto the wafer. Once activated, the symbol no longer mattered. The magic imbued whatever object held the hex. In this case, the wafer. It remained intact and didn't explode, nor did I get zinged.

Reiver cleared his throat. "It's not dangerous to you."

"So you keep claiming," I muttered. I grabbed the hexed wafer and took a big bite that put most of the smeared icing in my mouth. I chewed, my head tilted to the side, analyzing the taste and feeling. It might seem dangerous, but I was very good with most poisons. If it came from a plant, I could handle it.

"How long is this test going to take?" he complained as he checked his wristwatch.

"Until I'm satisfied it's not dangerous. If you don't like it, leave."

"I should," he grumbled, yet he leaned back and crossed his arms. "Would you feel better if I ate one?"

"Yes, actually."

"Hand one over then."

My oven timer dinged. "In a second. You'll be testing a cupcake soon as they cool enough the icing doesn't run all over the place."

My perfect little cakes emerged and went onto

racks as I readied myself for the next stage. I filled my piping bag, got my trays ready. My cooling racks had a hex to draw heat, which it funneled back to my stove, saving me in energy costs. Within minutes, the cupcakes were ready for icing. This would be the labor-intensive part. Each cupcake needed to have the hex drawn, but before I infused it, I had to drop icing on top of the hex to hide it. The existence of magic might be common knowledge, but witches guarded their secrets quite fiercely.

I started by frosting a single cupcake, quickly replicating the symbol, adding the magic, then a swirl of icing that didn't displace the symbol. I topped off with a sprinkle of cinnamon to make it extra potent and long lasting. I held up the finished product and scanned it, sensing the hex waiting within the treat.

He drawled, "Gonna hand it over or admire it all day?"

"Here you go." I lifted it to his mouth.

I half expected him to balk. Instead, he parted his lips and took a big bite. His eyes widened as he chewed, and he emitted a tiny groan of pleasure.

The man had a sweet tooth. He ate the whole thing. "That was fucking good."

The compliment pleased me even as my arrogance rose to the surface. "I know."

"Happy now? Did I pass your test?"

My lips curved. "I am not going to apologize for taking precautions."

"Satisfied I'm not trying to poison you?"

"Maybe." I played coy.

"You'll make more?"

"Yes. But I'm not sure who you think is going to buy them." A few days ago, I didn't believe in zombies. Pretty sure most people didn't. Still, his serious mien had me wondering if that would change.

His next statement confirmed it. "If the necromancer isn't stopped, the violence by the undead will escalate."

"If you say so." I reserved the right to be a little doubtful of his bold claim. Yes, I'd encountered a few zombies, which he'd easily taken care of. Did I really have anything to worry about?

"Make the cakes. Put a sign in your window."

"Saying what? A pumpkin spice cupcake a day keeps the zombies away?" I joked.

He didn't. "Yes."

I gaped. He couldn't be serious. Although, I had to admit, with Halloween coming, I could make some epic marketing graphics.

"Be careful." His parting words before he left.

I watched him go as I flipped my sign back to open. I needed to sell my current stock, or it would go to waste. A peek outside showed the crow gone. Good. Let it pick on someone else.

I brought my tray of cupcakes and icing out front and decorated them behind the tall counter while, at the same time, dealing with clients. Only once I had the entire tray ready did I pop into the kitchen to put them on the counter for the mass magical infusion.

One by one would take too long. I'd do the first batch in a single shot. But that required a little more juice than my body currently held. I had to resort to grounding myself. Literally.

I crouched to pull aside a tile on the floor. Under it was a hole into the crawl space where pipes and wiring ran, except for one spot. The tile I'd removed revealed a mound of dirt. Rich, dark soil replete with all kinds of living microbes and earthworms, a connection to Mother Earth.

I kicked off my left shoe—because hello, lefty—and dug my toes into the soil to commune with my goddess.

Hello, Mother. A fertile and bountiful day to you.

Daughter.

Speaking to the goddess brought an ecstatic shiver. We never said much, didn't have to. My goddess imbued every part of me. She knew me, body, soul, and thoughts. She understood my need and fed me power enough to fill the hexes with some left over.

More than usual.

Thank you, Goddess.

Beware. Her final word before fading.

As usual, her departure left me feeling a touch bereft, small, and sad I couldn't be with her forever. But it wasn't my time yet.

As the hexes ignited, I exhaled, opening my eyes. The cupcakes glowed, the green turning to yellow to silver. And done.

A smile tilted my lips. Praying always left me feeling at peace.

I set out the first tray of hexed cakes with a hand-written sign. I drew a terrible version of a stickman zombie, arms out, and called them Pumpkin Zombie Begone. I'll be honest, I didn't expect to move many of them.

As I started decorating the second batch, people wandered in and glanced with curiosity at my new offering. A few laughed as they congratulated me on starting my Halloween special early.

That first day, it took me until dinner time to sell half. Annie showed up while I was cashing out and saw my newest offering.

"What's this?" She pointed.

"New hex," I muttered.

"Zombie Begone." She rounded on me. "This is because of what happened with Ralph."

"Kind of." I bit my lip. I'd not yet told her about the attack at my place or Reiver. "The guy in that video dropped by my shop today."

"What?"

Annie's shrillness level rose as I told her everything. Including how Reiver had saved me from a marauding gang of the undead.

She hit me in the arm. "You asshole. Why didn't you call me?"

"I didn't want to bring any trouble to the farm."

Her glare proved she didn't care about my altruism. "I would burn that farm and everything on it if it would help you."

"I know." I did know because I'd do the same for her. We'd been friends forever. Met in kindergarten. She was closer to me than anyone, even my own family.

"No more trying to be a hero. If you see zombies, or hot guys in leather coats, you need to call me, ASAP." She slapped her hands together in punctuation.

"Yes, ma'am."

"I'm having a zombie cupcake," she declared, grabbing one.

"Take all of them. I was just going to freeze the leftovers." Quickies for emergencies.

"Mmm. Nummy," she declared, licking her fingers.

I glanced her over with a witchy eye, noticing the slight haze of magic as the hex settled. I wondered if the wafer I'd eaten remained active. "How come you're here? I'm not due for a delivery."

"Does a bestie need a reason to pop in unexpectedly?" she asked with an innocence I didn't believe for a minute.

My gaze narrowed. "Spill."

"A curio shop in Little China was robbed." And by little, she meant it. It consisted of literally three buildings on a third of a block.

"And?"

"All the charms warding against the dead were stolen. Their security footage showed one disguised person and a gang of goblins."

"Still don't see why the interest."

"The curio shop had security in the form of troll. The goblins ate it."

No one ate troll, not even goblins, unless they didn't care about taste. "You think it's the ones missing from my bin?"

"Could be."

"Did you see one with a scar over its eye?"

"The footage was grainy."

"How do you know it's not a fake?"

She shrugged. "I don't, but in case it wasn't, I checked it out. While the goblins ate the big dude, the person with them stole all the charms against the undead."

"Zombies..." I muttered.

"The goblins most definitely were, but not the thief. That was their puppet master. I did a bit of research on the undead and, apparently, they can only be created by a necromancer."

That brought a chill. "According to Reiver, you're right." I quickly explained what I'd learned from Reiver and finished with, "It's kind of scary that a necromancer is stealing protection we can use against their undead minions."

"Meaning they're planning ahead. But we're onto them. Don't worry. I'll figure out a plan." A terrifying statement. Annie reached for a lemon-curd-filled cupcake I'd made in the off chance my former goblin occupants returned. "So when do you think you'll see this Reiver guy again?"

"Never, if I had to guess. He's not the friendly sort."

My friend uttered a long sigh. "Those are the best kind."

"Only in books," I replied wryly. Annie did love reading romance, even as she didn't date. Not since the jerk who hurt her.

"The strong, silent, gruff type make the best kind of lovers. They're loyal. Passionate. And just plain yum," Annie declared.

"I'm not interested in dating him." Or anyone else for that matter.

"Tick-tock," she clucked. "I'm ready to be an aunt before I'm too old."

I grimaced. Talk about guilting me. But I let her because Annie couldn't have kids, and I had promised her she could live vicariously through me. "Can't we just get a dog?"

"I can't teach a dog curse words."

"Nor will you teach any child of mine," I admonished.

"Not in front of you, of course," she said with a roll of her eyes. "Now come on. Let's split and get you back to the farm. I left a pot of stew on, and I made bread this morning."

Only an idiot would say no to that.

Knowing my schedule, she didn't argue when I went to bed early. Tired, yet unable to sleep, I tossed and turned, my thoughts full of Reiver. Blame Annie. She'd dropped hint bombs all evening.

Is he built? Like a tank.

Deep voice? Enough to make me shiver.

Did you want to kiss him? Yes. But I doubt I'd get another chance.

CHAPTER

ELEVEN

THE NIGHT TOOK FOREVER TO PASS. EVERY TIME I MANAGED
to drop off into sleep, I startled awake, convinced I'd
heard something. At 4 a.m. when my alarm went off, I
was pleased to note I remained zombie—and Reiver
—free.

Given the early hour, I booked an expensive Uber
back to my shop rather than wake Annie.

The streets were calm. No sirens pierced the night.
Perhaps Reiver had exaggerated. My town wasn't in
danger.

My shop appeared just as I'd left it, and still
missing its goblins. I started my day making my usual
stuff. While it cooked, I put up the posters I'd created
the previous night with Annie while drinking a bottle
of wine. We'd had a giggling good time making the
marketing graphics: shambling zombies under a
partially clouded-over moon, heading for screaming
humans, while those eating cupcakes were left alone.

In retrospect, it might have been a tad explicit. Too late. I puttied the posters to the window and got to work.

My posters must have been a hit, because of the seventy-one cupcakes I made—the seventy-second having had an unfortunate accident that not even a one second rule could have saved—sold out before lunch.

It turned out my clever marketing was only part of the reason for my sudden success. Apparently, the night before a video had emerged of a zombie attack that happened at the bus station. A crew of shambling zombies—so decayed a few dropped limbs as they shuffled–attacked those waiting for their ride. They swarmed and grabbed anything that moved for a bite. The screaming had me wincing. In a stroke of luck, no one died, but people were being quarantined.

The bus depot was shut down pending an investigation. The news outlets downplayed the zombie angle, claiming a group of people high on drugs got frisky. A few people screamed about the dead people, but a lack of evidence had them written off as mental health issues.

Not everyone believed the media's downplaying. Some people decided it was better safe than sorry and bought my Pumpkin Zombie Begone treats. I made more cupcakes during my lunch, and they got snatched as fast as I could make them. Before five, I'd sold out and had to turn people away.

The next day, I dropped some of my less popular

items to make three times as many cupcakes and called in Bethany, an older woman who'd retired and only wanted occasional work. I needed an extra set of hands. Even with her helping in the front so I could bake in the back, I sold out, and my shop got busier. For the first time ever, I had a line out the door and I had to resort to store-bought ingredients because Annie ran out.

By day three, I taught the only other Earth Witch in town how to make the Zombie hex. She wove the spell into her bread. It eased the pressure for about two days until the most heinous attack by the zombies occurred at an old age home. All the residents and staff had been taken. People lost their minds and panicked.

Police and volunteers had been dispatched, looking for the aging relatives. So far, no sign other than the grainy videos from the hallways of the home, where people were herded outside and not seen again.

The anxiety in the population erupted as everyone sought to protect themselves. The lineup for my shop snaked down the street and held the fearful—along with those looking to profit by reselling my four-dollar cupcakes for crazy sums. It led to a limit on how many zombie-hex items people could buy at a time. No more than four. Even then, I sold out too quick. Those who couldn't get any turned ugly and sent Bethany home in tears.

That was the point where I locked up my shop. I'd been verbally abused to the point I didn't want to help people anymore. I hid in the kitchen, mixing up batches of simple sugar cookies, trying to remind myself folks were scared. Still didn't give them a right to be mean.

A knock at the back door drew my attention. As if I'd open it.

Tap. Tic. Tic. Tap.

Annie's secret code. She'd been picking me up and taking me home every day but only once she'd installed bars on my main floor windows and plywood over the bay one—which led to my neighbor freaking out about property values. In the morning, I took a taxi to my shop. A lot of precaution for nothing. I'd not seen any zombies since the group that attacked my house. But in annoying news, the crow by my shop appeared to have a pal living on my street. I swear the ugly bird watched me as I rushed into my house at night.

I quickly opened the back door of my store to my friend. "I thought you weren't supposed to come until tomorrow."

"Bethany called because she felt bad for leaving you. Thought you could use a hand, and I hit the organic food store supplies." She'd reversed her over-sized truck into one end of the alley. It wouldn't stop determined people. I kept watch as she loaded the dolly but saw nothing but a feathery blob perched on the roofline. Once she wheeled the load inside, I locked the door.

As we unpacked the items, Annie exclaimed, "I

can't believe people are literally camped out on your sidewalk."

"You know how folks get around pumpkin spice season." I tried to joke, but Annie knew full well why I was being mobbed.

"This shit with the zombies is getting crazy."

"Blame social media. They're making it worse."

"They stole an entire old folks' home. It doesn't get any worse."

I wrinkled my nose. "Which doesn't make sense. Why go after our most frail? And what about the bus station? Their targets have no rhyme or reason." I'd also seen a video supposedly taken in a church parking lot after bingo night, but I had my doubts about its authenticity.

"Aren't you paying attention? It makes perfect sense," Annie, my conspiracy queen, claimed. "It's not just those two places. You forgot about Second Chances and the curio shop. Also, last night the bridge at Madison Creek somehow collapsed and rumor has it there are a few roadblocks keeping traffic from leaving town."

"Probably because of an accident.

"Bullshit! We're being isolated."

"Oh." Blame anxiety and fatigue for not cluing in. "But why?"

"You should ask the hunk who taught you the zombie spell."

"I can't. I don't know where he is." I'd not seen Reiver since the day I learned the hex. I could only assume he'd yet to find the necromancer given the zombie activity.

More worrisome was the fact the necromancer appeared to be growing his troops. Why else take the old folk? Would they pick us off one by one?

Annie stayed to help, handling the clients in the store while I baked my ass off in the back. She was better at the whole getting-people-to-behave thing than me and thicker skinned than Bethany.

I kept one foot almost constantly in dirt, and apparently my goddess approved of my actions because she kept me well fed with her power.

Despite our hard work, we ran out of cupcakes midafternoon, and I was done for the day. Annie drove me home and saw me inside, once more attempting to get me to go home with her despite my new security.

"I'll be fine. Nothing's happened in days," I argued. Besides, it was much cheaper and easier to commute from my place to the shop.

"Fine my ass. Where's the scythe I gave you?"

Honestly? Hiding in the hall closet. Rather than admit that, I held up a bag and shook it. "I have zombie-repelling wafers!" I'd used a burning tool to etch the hex into the surface before activating it. It made them lower calorie for those watching their weight.

"Those only protect you from being seen by zombies. They're not the only threats out there."

"The world has always been a dangerous place. My

goddess will protect me." And if she didn't, I'd become a part of her.

"Ugh, you're so stubborn. Call me if you need me." Annie hugged me tight before leaving with her own box of cupcake protection. According to her, magic tasted better with icing.

Despite my exhaustion, I hexed my front door, back door, and boarded-over bay window. The only three remaining spots zombies could use to enter. I gave them enough juice to hopefully last until morning.

Or not.

Around 9 p.m., as I fetched myself a glass of warm milk, a scratching at the back sliding door had me pursing my lips. I'd drawn the curtains for privacy and had no way of seeing the other side. Smart women didn't investigate spooky noises at night, not when they were safe inside their homes.

Scratch. Mewl. As if a kitten. Probably a ploy.

Open it. It sounded like my goddess, and yet I didn't have a foot in the dirt.

Daughter.

The familiar shiver saw me set my glass down and pull back the curtain. Nothing stared back at me. The rear porch light refused to come on. None of my solar lights appeared to be active either.

Not a good sign and yet my foot dislodged the broomstick I'd cut down as my security. Dumb. Dumb. Yet, my goddess wanted me to open it. She wouldn't ask if it weren't important. Still, I went at it cautiously.

With a frying pan in hand, I grabbed the handle and eased the sliding glass door open. A goblin tumbled in, hitting the floor in a heap.

Expecting it to attack, I held the frying pan over it, only to frown. I didn't get a bad vibe from it.

The breeze from the open door reminded me to slam it shut. I shoved the wooden stick back in the track before I dropped to my haunches to roll over the little creature with a scar above its eye. I recognized it from my dumpster. Somehow the goblin found its way to me.

It blinked its eyes at me, the clearness easing my worry. It wasn't a zombie.

"What happened to you?" I muttered, checking it for damage. It appeared uninjured, if almost unconscious. I rose to gather a few things.

The clean and fluffy tea cloth I offered was taken with grateful eyes and wrapped around a small green body.

"May I?" I asked before lifting it to the table.

At its assent, I placed the goblin on a fabric placemat then offered tidbits of food. The creature ate slowly, which worried yet wasn't what chilled me the most.

I murmured, "What happened to you? Where are all your friends?"

The goblin croaked, "Gone."

CHAPTER

TWELVE

OKAY, SO COLOR ME SURPRISED. I DIDN'T EXPECT THE GOBLIN
to speak. I recoiled and gaped. It kept eating.

Maybe I'd misunderstood and thought it said a
word. "What did you say?"

For a second, it ignored me. It took a drink of the
water I'd given in my smallest measuring cup then
clear as a bell said, "Friends gone. Dead. Not dead."

Well.

The unexpected speech had me sitting down hard
on my stool. "What happened?"

"Taken. Bad magic." Stilted speech, the words
heavily accented, but more than I ever expected.

"Taken by who?"

"Bad magic," it repeated.

"You escaped?" I asked instead.

It nodded. "Mungo tricky."

"Mungo is you?" I pointed.

It nodded.

"I'm Mindy."

"Cakey."

"Yes, I make the cakes, but my name is Mindy."

"Cakey," it offered with a nod.

I could live with it. "Why did you come looking for me?"

"Good magic. Protect."

Maybe now I could, but I'd failed Mungo and its tribe by letting them be taken in the first place. "Hey, do you know where the others are? Can you help me find them? Maybe we can rescue them."

"No rescue." Mungo shook its head. "Dead. Not dead."

"Are they zombies?"

Mungo blinked.

I tried to think of another way of saying it. "Want eat Mungo?" I mimed, chewing my arm.

The goblin nodded. "Dead. Not dead."

Meaning it was too late for them, but we might still be able to stop the necromancer before anyone else got caught. "Listen, I know you must have been incredibly scared, but I could really use your help. If we can find the bad magic, we can stop it."

"Not scared." Mungo puffed its little green chest.

"Of course, you weren't. You are so very brave. Which is why you'll lead the way when we are ready to get rid of the bad magic."

"Lead?" Mungo paused eating and stared at me.

"Uh, yeah?"

It nodded. "Lead. Bad magic."

I almost clapped in glee, only to realize I couldn't go after the necromancer with just a goblin as backup. I'd need help.

Only two people came to mind. Annie, who would totally want to come on a dangerous mission, and Reiver, who actually knew what to do.

How could I find the latter?

On a hunch, I marched to my front door, opened it, and stood framed in the light. I glanced around and saw nothing. Didn't expect to, but anyone out there watching me would notice.

If anyone watched.

I waved both arms and uttered a high-pitched whistle. It drew attention. A flutter from the roof had me looking upward to see a swooping crow.

Oh no, not again.

As I slammed the door shut in the bird's face, I could only hope I'd not attracted the attention of something nefarious. Just in case, I armed myself with a vine garrote, donated by Vinny, and I fetched my scythe—the blade wept with the dry tears of all the crops it had severed. Poor wheat, like other short-lived vegetation, never stood a chance to be more.

I returned to the kitchen and waited with my new pal Mungo, who'd burrowed into my napkin holder for a snoring nap.

An hour I waited, going on the second. I yawned. Reiver wasn't coming.

I left my sleeping goblin on the table and headed upstairs for bed. I barricaded my door as a precaution.

Put a few tippy items under my bedroom window, which didn't have bars, and went to bed, one hand on my scythe.

I woke at dawn to a drawled, "You wanted to see me?"

THIRTEEN

Dɪᴅ I ᴘᴀɴɪᴄ ᴀ ʙɪᴛ ᴀɴᴅ sᴡɪɴɢ ᴍʏ sᴄʏᴛʜᴇ ᴡɪʟᴅʟʏ ʙᴇꜰᴏʀᴇ realizing my intruder was Reiver? Oh, heck yeah, I did. In my defense, he shouldn't have been in my room.

I managed to not kill him, mostly because he blocked my swing with his sword. *Clang.* The vibration went up my arm and into my teeth and destabilized my leaf bed. For the first time ever I got wet, going under before emerging with a screeched, "What the frig, dude?"

"Dude?" He arched a brow at me then eyed my choice of mattress. "Interesting."

"Don't you dare make small talk," I grumbled as I heaved my soaking-wet butt out of the tub. I propped the scythe by the side and wrung out my hair before snapping, "Why are you here?"

"Wasn't that the plan when you did that dance on your front stoop?"

"I expected you to knock." A glance showed my door remained barricaded. My window untouched. "How did you get in here?"

"I have my ways."

I glanced at the open bathroom door. "Don't tell me you squeezed through the window in my shower?"

"You shouldn't have stopped at barring just the first-floor windows. Do the second, as well, heavy on the iron and rune inset for ultimate protection."

"Why would I need bars? You're the first person who's ever broken into my house."

"I guess you're not counting the zombies from the other night," he chided.

"What kind of life do you lead that requires you to even think about that?" I squeaked.

"Nothing wrong with being cautious."

"I am not living in a fortress."

"Maybe you should," he argued.

It was too early in the morning for this.

Morning!

It hit me that dawn had already crested outside. "I'm late for work."

"About your shop..." He hesitated.

It led to me noticing the scuffs on Reiver's jackets, the bruising on his cheekbone, the scent of decay that clung to him. "You fought some zombies."

"Yeah. I did. Took care of them, problem being I got there too late."

My lips pursed. "Where did you arrive too late?" But I knew the answer. "They went after my shop?"

"Yes. Fuckers smashed in the front window and your display cases. Made a mess in the back, too."

I didn't need Annie and her conspiracies to growl, "The necromancer wants to stop me from making my hexed goods."

"Most likely."

"I'll clean up and be back in business within a few days," I promised hotly.

"A few days is probably all he needs."

"Then I guess we should stop him before that."

"There is no we," he retorted.

"Yeah, there is because I know where he is."

The man moved so quickly I almost swung with my scythe again. Maybe I did have the potential to be a bad-ass killer.

"Where?"

I licked my lips as I stared up at him, the scent of him distracting. "I don't have an actual location. But Mungo can lead us there."

He stared intently at me. "Who is Mungo?"

The goblin chose that moment to drop from the ceiling fan to Reiver's shoulder and place a sharp claw against Reiver's jugular.

The big man froze before arching a brow. "I take it this is Mungo."

"Yes. Mungo escaped the necromancer, but his tribe didn't."

Reiver pulled a piece of candy from his pocket and held it up for a second before tossing it to my dresser.

Mungo followed and greedily gobbled it, wrapper and all.

He eyed the goblin a little too intently for my liking. "If she escaped, then she can lead me there."

"She?"

"Don't tell me you didn't know."

I eyed Mungo and didn't see it. "If you say so."

"I do. Now if you don't mind, Mungo and I have a job to do." He held up more candy. "I've got a whole bag." The bribery had Mungo cocking her head in interest.

"I'm going with you," I declared.

Reiver snorted. "Like fuck you are."

"I want to help."

"I'm sure you do. But this isn't your kind of battle, Earth Daughter."

"You're not going without me." I didn't back down. The fact the necromancer came after me and my town made this personal. I might not be a fighter, but I also wasn't a coward.

"You're infuriating," Reiver complained, raking fingers through his hair.

"Takes one to know one," I taunted.

"That makes no sense."

"What doesn't make sense is why, despite you being you, I want to do this," I murmured before mashing my mouth to his. Blame the fact he smelled good or that, from the moment I'd woken to see him, I'd wanted to run my hands over his body.

Irrational, I know. Totally out of character. Not my type. Or the right time. I couldn't have even said why I did it.

Yet I kissed Reiver, and to my astonishment and delight, he kissed me right back.

FOURTEEN

Gʀᴜꜰꜰ ᴏɴ ᴛʜᴇ ᴏᴜᴛꜱɪᴅᴇ ʙᴜᴛ ꜱᴡᴇᴇᴛ ᴡʜᴇɴ ʜᴇ ᴋɪꜱꜱᴇᴅ. Rᴇɪᴠᴇʀ proved hard and soft when it came to embracing me. His mouth somehow managed to be tender and yet commanding at the same time.

His arms wrapped around me and held me on tiptoe that the kiss might keep going and going. Until a little goblin coughed something wet.

It ruined the mood, and we both stood apart suddenly, as if shy and wondering what the heck just happened.

I'd kissed him. Obviously. Enjoyed it immensely. But now felt awkward because I wasn't sure what it meant or what I wanted.

He appeared to immediately regret it. Or so it seemed. He stepped back and turned from me, crouching slightly to speak to Mungo while I touched my tingling lips as if I'd never been kissed before.

Not like that I hadn't.

Mungo had no interest in Reiver and his demands or questions. She bounced away with her thoughts on the matter. "I lead."

He turned to me with a scowl. "What's that supposed to mean?"

"I believe she thinks she is in charge of our mission."

"That's insane."

I shrugged. "Well, she is the only one who knows where we're going."

His jaw tightened. "I'm aware. And when is she planning on leading us there?"

"No idea. Guess we'll have to ask her."

Except, when we went looking for Mungo, she'd climbed into my dining room hutch, tucked into a soup tureen for a nap, and ignored Reiver's demand she "wake the fuck up."

"Leave her alone. She's probably had a rough couple of days." I tucked a tea towel around her.

"Days that will get rougher if the necromancer is allowed to keep acting unchecked." Reiver paced my living room with a scowl.

It was hard not be miffed that he'd so easily forgotten our kiss. Apparently, a one-sided attraction. It led to me being contrary to what he wanted. "Mungo is exhausted. She deserves a respite before we ask her to lead us into danger."

"She's a goblin."

"And? She's still a living being."

"You can't trust them."

"I am not a believer in generalizations but actions. So far, she's done nothing to warrant your suspicion." I chose to forget the earlier pranks.

"By the time she double crosses us, it will be too late."

"If you feel so strongly, you know where the door is."

He sat on the couch to glower some more.

"Don't be grumpy." I grabbed a tin from the sideboard and approached. "Take this as a moment to relax before the big battle. Toffee? I made them myself."

I held out a sticky piece, and rather than snare it, he grabbed at me, tugging me into his lap.

"Oh!" I exclaimed, and not just out of surprise at his action. I'd misjudged his aloofness if the erection poking my bottom was any indication.

"If we're going to talk, then it should be face to face," he insisted, staring into my eyes.

I didn't point out the chair across from him. "Toffee?" I said, pushing it against his lips.

He took the candy but also suckled my fingertips. His gaze never wavered from mine.

He chewed, and I couldn't resist kissing his lips. Then giving him my tongue, tasting the caramel stickiness, him, and the simmering passion.

When we were both panting and heated, he murmured, "What is it about you that I can't resist?"

I stroke my fingers over his angular cheek and

replied, "I could say the same. You're not my usual type."

"You're a distraction."

"Is that a bad thing?"

"I don't really fucking care. I can't think when you're around." An admission to melt me.

"Then let's not think."

"And what should we do instead?"

My lips curved. "I'm sure we can find something to do while we wait."

We kissed again, and his hands roamed this time, sliding under my loose shirt to skim over my flesh. Despite my enjoying the cradle of his lap, he slid me to the couch that he might better explore. He laid me back on the cushions, removing my shirt that he might caress and suckle my breasts.

I gasped and writhed as I clutched at his hair. My hips bucked as he palmed me through my slacks.

He pushed them down far enough to touch me. He found me wet and willing. I dragged him down for a kiss as he fingered me. I panted into his mouth as his thumb rubbed my clit. I clung to his shoulders as I rode his hand.

I could feel my climax rising, and I whispered, "I want you inside me." Wanted to feel the thickness of him.

"Come for me," he ordered. "Now."

How bossy.

How exciting. My body arched as I climaxed, my

pussy clenching his fingers, and he grunted as if having a mini orgasm of his own

His lips clung to mine as he drew out my orgasm. Who knows where things might have gone if Annie hadn't started pounding on my door?

CHAPTER
FIFTEEN

"MINDY! OPEN UP! MIN-N-N-D-Y!" ANNIE YODELED AS I scrambled off the couch.

There was nothing like getting caught with your pants down quite literally to fly into frantic mode. My cheeks heated as I righted my clothing, hoping I didn't have an after-orgasm face and that I'd left nothing unbuttoned.

The moment I unbarred the front door, Annie rushed in, exclaiming, "You'll never believe what happened."

For some reason my gaze slewed to Reiver on the couch, looking quite smug with himself. He deserved it. Usually, a guy had to work harder to get me to come hard like that.

It took effort to drag attention to my best friend. "What happened?"

"My animals. They're gone."

The words drew my attention, and I focused on Annie. "Excuse me, what did you say?"

"I didn't notice until like an hour ago on account Rusty didn't wake me up at the crack of dawn. I figured he croaked, or the foxes finally got him, only the entire coop was empty. As were my barn and the pastures!" Her hands waved to punctuate her panic.

"Where did they go? Was there any blood?" An animal attack of that magnitude seemed unlikely, not to mention scavengers tended to leave bodies behind.

"It is like they just wandered off. Every damned one of them! Betsy and Rory, Yumyum and Jus."

It always surprised me Annie named her animals knowing she'd eventually eat some of them. Then again, was I any different, lavishing my plants with attention only to harvest them at need?

The circle of life involved death because, in order for one living thing to survive, it had to consume the life of another. Animal or plant, we were all technically killers.

A morbid thought to have so I shoved it away. Now wasn't the time for maudlin introspection.

"They must have left some kind of tracks," Reiver interjected, rising from the couch and drawing Annie's attention.

Her eyes widened. "Holy shit, you're the hottie she was talking about."

He arched a brow at me.

"Keep your cool, Mr. I-Like-To-Keep-Private. I just told her a handsome stranger showed me a spell to repel zombies. She doesn't know you work for the CA as a zombie killer."

Annie blinked.

He grimaced.

I smirked. "Annie, meet Reiver. He's hunting the necromancer making the zombies. Reiver, my best friend, Annie, to whom I tell almost everything."

"Almost?" Annie protested.

"Do you really need to know Reiver and I were making out before you interrupted?" I dropped a nugget to divert her attention.

"Would you like me to leave for five minutes so you can finish?" she offered saucily.

Reiver groaned.

"Ooh, I'll give you ten if he promises to make that noise again."

Reiver growled. "This is not amusing."

"Maybe not to you." Annie grinned, but her lips fell a second later as she remembered her reason for coming. "Do you think they're in danger?"

"Honestly? We might need to watch out for Old MacDonald's army," I opined.

"Dammit. And Rory was just about ready for the butcher. He had the most bacony ass of all my hogs." She pouted.

"That's sick," I complained.

"It's called coping with reality. And don't deny it would have been delicious."

"I don't eat meat."

"But I do," Reiver interjected. "If we can find them

before the necromancer has a chance to change them, then I will expect you to share the bounty."

Annie stuck out her hand. "Deal."

I shook my head. "So you'll rush out to save a pig but not the old people taken last night."

"They're probably in the same place. Follow the one to find the other. Where is your farm?" he asked Annie. "We should go now before the trail weakens."

"Or we could wait for Mungo and let her lead us."

"Hold on, who is Mungo?" Annie asked.

It took a minute to explain, and for Annie to see the sleeping green critter before she was satisfied.

"Why won't she wake up?" Annie asked.

Reiver had a reply. "A goblin won't be woken before they're ready, especially once in a healing sleep, or I would have already had her leading us. Just in case, though, bring her along."

I opened my mouth to argue, only to realize he included me on his mission. "Sounds good."

"You'll need to bring your scythe."

A reminder I'd have to chop off zombie heads. Here was hoping I could act if needed rather than freezing.

"What do you have for a weapon?" he then asked Annie, who launched into a list of items she kept in the back of her truck. The tire iron, I understood. The axe and chain saw? What dark web conspiracy site had she fallen into this time?

Only after Reiver showed her his sword, which he somehow managed to keep sheathed in his long coat, did Annie drop her own bomb. "I can't believe you're working for the CA. My dad used to hunt for them, too."

I gaped. "Your dad? He was a farmer."

"He was by the time you knew me. He used to tell me stories as a kid. It's how he met my mom. She was a farmer like her dad. My grandpa apparently got eaten by some hobgoblins from the marsh, and my dad was sent to handle it. They fell in love and Dad retired from the CA and only did occasional jobs to help them out."

I pointed at her accusingly. "How is it I never knew this?"

Annie shrugged. "Used to be we had to keep it secret in case old enemies came looking, and honestly, I forgot. It's been a while since I've thought of him." Her father had died with her mom in a tragic car accident just after we finished college.

"You better not ever complain again about me keeping anything from you." I wagged my finger.

"I will complain. And you will berate me for the fact I never told you I have elf ancestry. But in the end, we'll still be best friends because we understand what it means to make a promise to someone."

I grimaced. "Sometimes I hate you."

"Because you love me."

I did.

Reiver eyed us and harrumphed. "Are you both done being sentimental? Grab the goblin. We should get going before the trail gets cold."

It took but a moment to snare the soup tureen,

secured with its lid, the steam cap open to ensure Mungo had air. As we marched out the door, I had to ask, "What makes you think there will be a trail? Won't they have loaded the animals onto a truck like they did the old people?" Some things even Reiver couldn't track apparently.

"Animals shed more than humans."

We exited to the day in full bloom, the sun shining, Vinny tanning in its vibrant rays. All my plants sucked in the nutrients of this beautiful day. The dichotomy of hunting for a zombie lair didn't escape me.

As we hit the curb, I noticed a motorcycle parked by Annie's truck. No surprise, Reiver straddled it.

"You riding with me?" He glanced back at the sliver of seat left for a passenger.

Before I could yell, "Yes!", and wrap my arms anaconda-style around him, Annie tugged me in the direction of her van. "Don't be silly. She's got Mungo to handle."

Never mind I could have placed the tureen on the front seat. It ended up on my lap, with me riding shotgun beside Annie.

An Annie in the mood to talk. "So, that's Reiver. Such a ray of sunshine. I can see why you like him."

"I don't like him," I sputtered.

"Please." Annie popped the P. "It's so obvious you have the major hots for him. And he's totally into you."

"Doesn't matter if he is or isn't. He won't be around long. From the sounds of it, his job has him moving around a lot."

"Don't be so sure. He could ask to be posted here. It's what my dad did before he finally retired."

"As if he'd want to make such a drastic change for someone he just met." It would be crazy and wild and romantic. For me? I just couldn't see it happening.

"Why are you hesitating about dating him?" Annie asked, driving her van as if it were a low-slung sports car. We took a corner on two wheels, and I leaned against the pull of gravity until we slammed back down with a thump.

"I'm not hesitating. He's not the dating kind." Fooling around, yes, but anything more? I retained enough wits to understand the spark between us would never become a full-fledged fire.

"What makes you think he isn't?"

I opened my mouth to speak, only to realize I had made a huge assumption. One that I clung to lest my poor heart get broken. "He's only here for the necromancer. Once that's taken care of, he'll leave."

"Don't be so sure of that."

Knowing her mom and dad fell in love at first sight, I saw why she might be hopeful in that respect. My parents? Hated each other. Arranged marriage to produce me, an Earth Witch who proved disappointing. It was only part of the reason why they'd divorced in my early teens and my mom moved to the opposite side of the country. Soon as I went to college, Dad disappeared, too. I occasionally got a card from them. I was petty enough not to reply. I also refused to participate in the breeding game some of the other magically inclined played. I'd rather marry for love.

My parents' relationship failed because they'd not had a bond that drew them together like Annie's parents had. A bond Annie seemed to think might be forming between me and Reiver.

A glance in the sideview mirror showed him riding behind, a half helmet on his head, sunglasses covering his eyes. Expression grim and intent. A true hunter. And me, a nurturer. It would never work.

"You're watching him again," Annie said as she noticed my glance.

"Just making sure he can keep up."

"Sure, you are. Admit it, you like the man."

"He's attractive, but we're too opposite," I argued.

"So were my parents."

"I don't know if I have it in me to be with a person long term." Even short term I had issues.

"We've been friends for how long?"

"That's different."

"Don't let your dysfunctional parents scare you off from something good."

"I should take heed since their partnership ended in divorce."

"Because your mom was a dippity cow who thought monogamy was ruining the planet. Can't blame your dad for telling her to take a hike."

Add in a child who was anything but remarkable and she'd had no reason to stay. My mother had been very free spirited. Too free. She died young because of it. Not of disease but from sleeping with the wrong sorceress's husband.

Annie wasn't done. "Forget about your mom."

"My mom has nothing to do with my life."

"Yeah, she does, because you're worried you're like her, that you'll get with one guy and get bored and run off."

"Everyone says I take after her."

"Maybe in looks and the fact you have Earth magic, but you're the girl who has roots. Like seriously deep ones. Do you really think you're the type to care if a relationship gets comfortable? That's your jam. The one thing you need around you at all times."

"Did you just call me boring?"

"No, just that you're not the type to ditch something because the initial excitement at getting it wore off. Look at us. How long we been friends?"

"I see your point, not that it matters. I'm not dating Reiver. We barely just met."

"And according to you already made out."

"I lied."

"Please. You totally did."

"What makes you say that?"

"I help animals breed for a living. I know," Annie confided.

I blushed hotly. For several minutes.

Annie tensed. "Almost there."

We drove past the fencing closing in her small ranch on the very outskirts of town. She'd held on tight to her agricultural zoning as the suburbs expanded. Manageable for one person with the occasional hand.

The pastures didn't hold any sheep. No cows grazed. We pulled into the gravel drive wide enough for several vehicles. We emerged to find the farm the quietest I'd ever heard.

Reiver parked and removed his helmet. He turned his head in a few directions before declaring, "Zombies took them."

"You're sure?" I asked because I didn't smell or sense a thing.

"I'm sure," he grumbled, disgruntled I'd even questioned.

"How could zombies take them without waking me up?" Annie shook her head. "Impossible. My animals do not like strangers. They would have lost their shit."

"Not if they were spelled to sleep." He dropped the suggestion, and I frowned.

"The size of the hex you're talking about—to cover the entire farm—it's just not feasible," I speculated aloud.

He had a counter argument. "It is doable if the spell was ingested, say via a contaminated water supply and placed on a timer ensuring everyone passed out at the same time."

"That's some complicated spell casting." I'd only rarely used timer hexes because they could be tricky to set off.

"It would explain why I heard nothing," Annie

remarked with a scowl. "Good thing I had the house on apocalypse lockdown." At my stare, she shrugged. "So I might not have mentioned when you were in that forest last spring collecting that special moss that I had the house outfitted with hurricane shields for the doors and windows. Just in case."

"Of what?"

"Well, zombies for one."

"You have a problem." I shook my head.

"Do I really? I mean those things probably saved my life."

"I'll agree they might have, but what about your massive stash of jarred preserves you keep in the basement?"

"I like my cupboards to be full."

"You have five thousand jars."

"Never know when I'll have a drought year."

Reiver's sharp whistle cut our conversation short. "Are you going to continue cackling like hens or provide meager assistance in finding the herd?"

"I'll help once you tell me how to figure out which way they went," Annie sassed.

"Can't have been far," I remarked as I recalled something Annie told me. "Didn't you say the roads out of town have been closed off for various emergencies?"

"Yes. All the main roads are. We're hemmed in rather tight." Her eyes widened as she suddenly realized what I was getting at. "Meaning there aren't many places you could hide a bunch of animals."

"By not many, I take it you know of a few we can investigate?" Reiver asked.

"I think we can do one better," I replied. "Given they were moving livestock, they have to be going somewhere big enough no one will notice, a place no one goes near, not even in passing."

Annie nodded and said, "Only one spot that could be. Flintstone Quarry."

CHAPTER

SIXTEEN

EVERYONE KNEW THE FLINTSTONE QUARRY. ABANDONED IN the eighties, it was a series of massive pits linked by narrow chasms. The kids called it Knock-off Baby Canyon. Nothing close to the real thing but fun to pretend. It shut down when the owner of the company fled the country after failing a series of inspections, which then led to the discovery of shady accounting practices.

Given the red tape surrounding the quarry, it was never reopened. It became a place to hang out for teens until the accident a few years back. The police report said the kids were partying and drinking, as teenagers are wont to do. During a game of truth or dare, a fifteen-year-old with way too much alcohol in his blood chose the dare. He climbed the steep cliff to dive in a waterlogged hole. It didn't end well for him or the three other kids that went drunk diving to save him. None of them were ever found.

The parents and town lost their grieving minds. *Shut it down!* The road into the quarry ended up barricaded. A fence with barbed wire was erected around the whole thing. People avoided it, claiming it was haunted.

Turned out they might be right. What a perfect lair for a necromancer looking to build an army out of the public eye.

And we were going to apparently drive right into it. The closer we got, the more it sounded insane.

"We need a better plan," I said.

Annie was in the driver's seat and Reiver in the passenger. With his giant legs, it would have been cruel for him to squish in the back. I sat in the rear, the soup tureen holding Mungo at my side. Panic lurked nearby, ready to pounce as my sudden burst of courage met reality.

"The plan is to use the element of surprise to attack," Annie replied with confidence.

"Just stay behind me and handle the stragglers," Reiver added.

"You expect three of us to handle an army of dead people?" Even if Reiver counted as almost three people on his own, the numbers didn't look good for us. If I were to count all the people missing from Second Chances, the farm, and the LTC facility, plus who knew how many others, that put us at a serious numbers disadvantage.

"The plan isn't to combat the zombies but the

necromancer. We go straight after him. Once he is dead, his constructs will lose their animation."

"Take out the big guy. Got it." Annie didn't appear to have any trepidation at all. On the contrary, she practically bounced with glee.

I was surrounded by heroes. I should be braver, but I still had questions, because I didn't want to be a blurb in the newspaper. *A local baker, who delighted hundreds with her confections, has been eaten by zombies. She should have stuck to making delicious treats.*

Despite the shining sun, it was a horrible day to die, hence why we needed to discuss the insanity a bit more. "I see a problem with the plan. What if you can't find the necromancer quickly and we're outnumbered by the brain-seeking undead?"

"Then we fight." A nonchalant reply by Mr. Arrogant in the front. He'd been a lot less confidant when his motorcycle refused to start back at the farm and he'd been forced to bum a ride in Annie's truck.

"I love how you don't sound bothered by that," I grumbled. "We might be talking like a hundred zombies."

"Possibly more," he agreed. "So ensure each blow counts. Make good use of your scythe."

I blinked. "You want me to behead people?" I kept trying to forget the fact that in a fight I'd have to act. He expected me to wield a blade and remove someone's head. "I feel sick."

Annie was the one to snort. "Don't pussy out now.

Just remember, they're already dead. If you don't decapitate them, then you might join them."

Her advice didn't help my roiling stomach or conscience. "They're still people. They didn't ask to be zombies."

Reiver turned in his seat to fully eye me. "And what would you suggest we do instead? Have a conversation? Perhaps wrestle them one by one into submission to do what? There is no cure."

I slumped. "I understand we have to kill them, but could we at least not act so callous about it?"

Reiver's expression shut down, as in it went fully blank. "As part of my job, I can't afford to care too much. It interferes with my task."

"Well, don't let me get in the way of that," I snapped.

"You won't."

For some reason his words hurt, and like any wounded beast, I lashed back. "Really regretting my recent desperate choice. Should have bought new batteries."

It took Annie trying to muffle a snort for his eyes to widen and affront to drop his jaw. He got the insult and didn't like it, judging by the narrowing of his eyes.

Annie tsked. "Now, now, children. No more fighting. Kiss and make up."

"I'd rather kiss a zombie." I leaned back and folded my arms.

I fully expected Reiver to say something snarky.

His lips twitched. "That bad? Guess I'd better work on my technique for the next time."

"There won't be a next time!" I huffed.

"There will be. After we've dealt with the necromancer."

"You know, Mindy is right," Annie interjected. "We shouldn't drive right up to the front door and announce ourselves. I've got an idea." She suddenly veered off the road, the rutted track obviously not in use given how much we jostled.

"Is this supposed to be a shortcut?" Reiver queried.

"Not shorter, more of a back door into the quarry." Annie held the jostling steering wheel with two hands.

If I remembered correctly, the trail went out of use for a good reason. "I thought this road stopped being used because of the creek?" A few years ago, torrential rain over a period of several days turned a once gentle creek into a raging river that only ever subsided, and never dried up, because of the new paths it cut.

"It's not that high. We should be fine. I got the exhaust vented above the cab." Meaning she intended to plow right through it.

"I don't know if that's a good idea, Annie. I thought the last car that tried it got swept down river."

"Because Simmons is an idiot who drove one of those new micro, good-for-the-environment cars. In other words, tiny and the motor run by a hamster in a wheel. Even a small puddle would have drowned it. My truck can handle it."

Reiver glanced back at me. "Don't be afraid."

"I'll be scared if I want to." Because, apparently, I possessed the only brains of the group.

The sparse forest opened into a scrubby shoreline, jagged to accommodate the water flowing through it. Water that appeared rather high and angry despite the dancing beams of light over its rippling surface.

Rather than cautiously gauge the situation, Annie gunned her truck and hurtled for the river. I grabbed the soup tureen and held it as we jostled and bounced before slamming into the water with a splash that sent a wave over the windshield.

Annie yodeled, "Ya-hoo! Let's go, Big Fred." The name of her truck. The 6.7 Diesel Hemi roared as we shoved through.

We were going to make it. Halfway across, the water sluiced from either side as we cut through it.

Another yell emerged from Annie. "That's it, Fred, my lovely hunk of metal l—"

The wave of water came out of nowhere.

CHAPTER
SEVENTEEN

THE UNEXPECTED TORRENT SLAMMED INTO US AND CARRIED us like a piece of flotsam. It jerked us around hard enough Mungo woke from her nap.

She emerged from the tureen with a stretch. It took only one look for her to squeak, "Bad. Water." She climbed me like a tree to nest in the hair at my nape. Cute if a bit weirdly scaly against my skin.

"What do we do?" Annie yelled, still holding the steering wheel as if it made a difference as we spun in the torrent.

"Where does this river flow?" Reiver asked suddenly.

"Uh-oh." My helpful reply. The new channel cut by the creek turned into river, which became a waterfall that plunged more than a hundred feet into the quarry.

"The quarry, oh shit!" Annie fumbled at her seatbelt. "We need to get out of the truck before we get swept over the edge."

The electrical still worked for the moment, and the windows whirred down. Well, the front ones did. Mine stopped halfway.

Reiver noticed and growled, "Once I'm out, climb through the seats and follow me."

Easier said than done. Reiver heaved himself out the window as I wiggled through between the seats into the front. I was halfway over when we hit something hard.

The truck jolted and spun, whipping me to the side. Annie shrieked, and I finished slipping face first into the foot well. With my face pressed to the rubber mat, it took me a second to recover my stunned senses. By the time I reacted to Reiver's yelling, it was too late.

A glance to the window showed Reiver gone. Probably flung off with the impact. Hopefully he'd get to shore. As for me—

The truck hit the edge of the waterfall before I could escape.

Down, down I went, goblin and all.

Splash!

The impact didn't slam me as hard as expected, the water somewhat softening the blow. It filled the cab of the truck quickly and would drown me if I didn't find my way out of the sinking death trap.

Mungo clung tight to my hair as I reached through bubbling water for the window frame. I hauled myself through it and pushed up—or so I hoped. I couldn't tell which direction I faced.

I kicked and pushed with my arms until I reached the surface, my wet face emerging to be embraced by glorious air. I heaved a breath, and another, as I treaded water.

Mungo poked her head out of my nest of hair and gasped. She then kindly spat and gargled by my ear. Lovely. It rinsed off as I swam, doing an easy breaststroke to the shore. As I made my way, I glanced around for my companions.

The constant splash of falling water meant I couldn't hear them, but I did spot Annie jumping at the top of the cliff, waving her arms. By her side was Reiver. I could just imagine his grim expression.

At least we all lived. For now. I couldn't help the ominous dun-dun-dun music playing in my head, for while they remained at the top of the cliff, I found myself alone at the bottom, weaponless. I'd lost every single thing I brought with me except for my zip-up sweater, which did its best to bog me down.

I pushed a little magic into the material. The hemp-based threads responded to my request to lighten my load. It became easier to remain afloat.

The water ran too deep for me to walk to shore, so I swam to the stony edge and gripped it. Mungo launched herself from my neck and sniffed suspiciously at the ground.

"Dead. Not Dead," Mungo declared as I hoisted myself out of the water.

Great, we'd found the zombies. Not so great, finding myself alone in a quarry *with* the zombies. A glance upward showed Reiver and Annie gone, most likely making their way to me. So what should I do? Stand and wait for them, or go scouting? The latter seemed foolish. What if I ran into a zombie? I'd lost my scythe. All that remained of my defensive stash was a soggy garrote that I hoped to not use because that would mean getting close.

I did have one positive thing, though. In my inner coat pocket, sealed within a Ziploc bag, a magical aid that remained dry. As part of my preparation, I'd made some anti-zombie wafers because my ingestible magic didn't care if I used a cupcake. It was the hex that counted. It should be noted we'd all eaten one before setting out, all but Mungo who'd been asleep. Yet I felt a need to reinforce that magic.

I unsealed the bag to reveal the wafers. They were a little bit squished, but the magic remained active.

One went into my mouth. I extended another to Mungo. "Eat it. It will help with zombies." As if Mungo needed a reason to swallow it whole.

As I went to put the bag into my pocket in case we needed them later, Mungo snatched it and dumped them all in her mouth.

"No!" I reached too late. The goblin ate them all and burped. "You shouldn't have done that," I chided.

Mungo rubbed her belly. "Hungry."

"That much hex at once isn't good for you!"

"Mungo fine. Mungo—" The goblin's face

contracted. Her nose twitched. Fur sprouted. Despite the grumbling, Mungo flipped from goblin to furry cutie with big emerald eyes and the most adorable pink nose.

"No!" She shook a cuddly fist, and I just wanted to hug her and love her.

Instead, I smirked. "Guess that will teach you."

Mungo adorably kicked at a stone with her paw, and her big eyes blinked.

So cute. Hopefully, despite her current form, she'd still be invisible to zombies.

Which reminded me of the situation. I'd ended up in the far end of the quarry where an excavated pit accumulated water. Given it never overflowed, it was surmised that an underwater tunnel must be helping to keep the small but deep lake level.

A worn track, about fifteen feet wide, ringed the pit. A dirt and stone ramp sloped into the body of water. It used to allow trucks up and down the hole with their rocky prizes. I'd seen the pictures taken before the quarry was abandoned. Its loss almost shut down the entire town. It took a while before the town recovered, mostly due to a tech firm having chosen to headquarter in the many vacant buildings downtown. Crypto Backo turned a dying town into a thriving one, their large, well-paid workforce bringing other businesses into the area.

A history lesson that did nothing to help me recall the exact layout of the quarry. If memory served me right, there were more than nine massive canyons linked by crevices to avoid having too many ramps. The main ramp, the one that could accommodate two lines of traffic going to the surface, being on the opposite side. The most common route in and out. Also probably where I'd find the necromancer. However, it wasn't the only path.

Most likely, Annie and Reiver went for the back exit, the emergency route upwards that usually had the word sketchy attached to it. If they took it, then it would dump them one canyon away from my current location.

By the time they'd found the route and made it down, I'd have gone stir-crazy. I had to do something. Reconnaissance by myself seemed risky. Best I go and meet my allies and together we'd go looking for the necromancer.

First things first. Get out of this mini canyon. "Ready to go?"

"Up." The adorable Mungo chose to ride on my shoulder. "Lead. Way." She pointed to the only way out of this section of the crevice to the next. I kept an eye out for anything I could use for a weapon because I honestly had no clue what I'd do if confronted.

Reiver might have had a point when he tried to leave me behind. Asset or liability, so far, I'd yet to figure out which category I fell into.

As we neared the crevice, Mungo hid in my hair with a softly chittered, "Bad."

The warning made me slow my steps. I halted

entirely as I caught a whiff of decay. Strong, putrid. Something dead was obviously inside the gap.

It proved hard to pierce the shadows in the darkened gash. The angle of the sun didn't illuminate the large, shadowy pockets along its length very well.

Moving shadows.

As I watched, a dark spot shifted, and I realized bodies filled those spaces.

Zombies. Not just the human kind either. A cow's rump stuck out from the group for a second.

Uh-oh. I'd found part of Annie's farm, and it appeared we'd gotten here too late.

My first instinct? Turn around and march back, but the backdoor ramp was in the next section, not to mention, even if I retreated, I'd find no escape. I had to forge forward. If the hexed wafer worked, they'd never see me.

Gulp.

I wish Mungo hadn't eaten my whole stash because I craved another.

I'll be fine. I took a deep breath.

Focus. Relax. No panicking. Even breaths in and out. I centered myself before taking a step right down the middle of that stone alley, wide enough for a single truck and not much more. A glance overhead showed sheer stone. I'd seen the demolition movie for the creation of these narrow crevices. Carefully placed charges, followed by the mining of the rock.

At least they'd excavated enough I could walk in sunshine as opposed to in a dark tunnel. One of the canyons could only be accessed by the Hell Hole. What the kids called it because the wind that whistled through sounded like a demonic whisper. Closed down because of the issues they'd had with trucks breaking down in the middle of it. And the drivers who didn't go missing emerged traumatized, the lawsuits and settlements also part of why the quarry failed.

A few strides and I came abreast of the first cluster of bodies tucked away from the direct light. Their writhing shapes clenched my stomach, and I couldn't help but stare as I marched quietly past. Noticed the thin, white hair of old people. The bright pastels some of the women wore. The chickens milling around at their feet.

And there was Rory. Alas, he'd never become epic bacon.

As I stepped past, I kept expecting them to suddenly swivel and focus on me. To fixate with a stare before lunging at me with clacking teeth.

Not one glanced my way. It reassured me less than you'd expect.

Mungo clung tight, head swinging to watch both sides. Every single pocket of shadow held zombies, the lot of them in some kind of jittery napping mode, the cow's tongue lolling as it swayed in place.

They ignored me, I ignored them, even as I wondered what Reiver would do. Even he might have difficulty fighting against this many.

Three-quarters of the way through, I could see the way the other side open up. The pit beyond was filled with sunlight. I thought we were going to be okay. I really, really did.

And then someone stepped into view and said, "How nice of you to drop in. My pets could use a snack."

Uh-oh.

EIGHTEEN

Seeing someone in the quarry, an out-of-place stranger, had me almost peeing my pants. "Who are you?"

"As if you don't know," was the sassy reply from the woman confronting me. From this distance, she appeared my age or a bit younger with a curvy figure and long red hair—with a body wave I'd never achieved in any of my failed perm attempts. It was why I now stuck to a simple bob.

"Are you security for the quarry?" I played super dumb and pretended to not notice the zombies flanking her. The human ones wore hoods over their heads, mostly likely as protection from the sun. At her heels were Annie's baby goats, still in their pajamas.

Sadness.

Mungo hid under my hair, hopefully out of sight. I tried to look as benign as possible. "Sorry if I'm trespassing. It was just such a nice day for a swim."

"It's a perfect day for all kinds of things, although I'm surprised to see you here. Shouldn't you be in the kitchen making cupcakes?"

Should I be flattered she recognized me? "Even bakers need a day off."

"And you chose to use that time to come looking for me. Congrats, you found me," the woman sang and did a pirouette.

"You're the necromancer?" A heavily skeptic note filled the query.

"Let me guess, they told you it would be a man."

I nodded.

"Yet here I am!" She extended her arms in a *ta-da!* motion.

Still, I had a hard time accepting her claim. Blame my preconceived notion of a necromancer. For one, she didn't wear black or even a long mermaid-type dress. The woman sported a floral summer dress cinched at the waist, flaring at her hips. Her hair was pulled back with a clip, and she wore black ballerina flats. She appeared ready for the country club, not raising the dead.

"You don't look like a necromancer," I blurted out.

"Such an old-school title. I prefer the title Puppet Mistress." She waved her hand, and the zombies against the wall took one step forward and halted, wavering in place, waiting for a command. Want to bet it would involve me?

"Why are you doing this? What are you hoping to accomplish?"

She appeared positively beautiful as she smiled and said, "World domination, of course. It's time us gingers showed everyone we're not to be trifled with." Announced with a fling of her hair.

It sounded ridiculous, and yet I had no doubt she believed every word of it. Worse, she would act upon it. "Shouldn't you have chosen, I don't know, a city with an airport at least or maybe a military base? Our claim to fame is our peach pie." Kind of ironic considering we had to import the peaches.

She waved a hand. "Goes to show how little you know."

"What I know is it's not nice to kill people just so you can turn them into your undead army."

She uttered a delightful titter at odds with her actions. "Bah, as if anyone cares. I mostly used those society no longer had any use for. You should thank me for making them less of a burden and repurposing them. Reduce, reuse, recycle." The occasional way she sang her words gave me shivers.

"Those people had families who cared for them." I tried to appeal to any rational part of her that might exist—buried deep.

Rather than get angry, she scoffed. "Really, are you trying to make me feel guilty? Because it won't happen. I am one hundred percent aware and satisfied with my actions thus far. And I'll go even further to achieve my goals."

"Not if I stop you." I took a few steps in her direction, praying the hex still hid me.

None of the zombies turned to watch my path.

The necromancer, puppet mistress, crazy-as-a-loon lady, smirked. "Look at you, acting all cocky."

Apparently, my act worked. She didn't see the trembling within. I angled my chin. "I know you're afraid of me."

"You?" She sounded astonished.

"Why else send zombies to attack my house and destroy my shop?" I blustered.

"That wasn't for you. I wanted to draw out your sword-wielding friend. He's a lovely specimen. Someone fresh and strong like him would be a perfect addition for my final coup."

The idea of Reiver being zombified horrified. "You leave him alone."

"Or what? Going challenge me to a bake off?" she mocked.

"When I'm done with you, you'll be wishing I'd stuck to frosting," I threatened, kicking off my shoes to dig my bare toes into the ground. With the soil devoid of life, I didn't get the hoped-for jolt. The rocks in this area formed a hard shell that kept me from the living, breathing vibrancy of my goddess.

"Foolish little baker, you should have stuck to doing what you knew best. Such a shame. I'd planned to keep you around. I hear your red velvet cupcakes are to die for. However, I can't have you interrupting my triumph."

"Too bad." I was mere paces away from her and feeling more confident by the second. "I won't let you get away with this." I got almost within reach, and still she acted as if I wasn't a threat. Maybe I wasn't. I'd yet to find any plants to use against her, and I needed something if I wanted to cast a hex.

"Silly little Earth witch. You think you're so clever with your look-away spell. You are so uninformed. I am the puppet master, which means, even though my pets can't see you, I can. Want to play?" She lifted her hand, the fingers splayed wide, and I heard the moan and shuffle as the dead bodies moved away from the wall, braving the sun.

Trepidation formed a ball in my gut. "You won't get away with this."

"Said every want-to-be hero ever. But haven't you noticed—because Hollywood sure has—the good guys don't always win. Catch."

She tossed something at me, and I reached to grab it out of reflex, only to utter a sharp exclamation as a small water balloon burst, spraying me with liquid.

The zombies' teeth began to clack.

"The thing about your hex," the necromancer announced, "is it hides the scent of your blood but no one else's. And guess what you're wearing?"

I gagged, which did nothing to halt the zombies shuffling in my direction.

"Good-bye, little baker. Hope you enjoy being on the opposite end of the gastronomic experience."

With that, the necromancer disappeared. The zombies at her back flowed around her, aiming for me.

I retreated but had nowhere to go. A ring of the undead closed in.

I needed a plan, one that didn't involve pissing my pants.

"Ideas?" I muttered to Mungo.

She emerged from my hair to jump to the ground. Mungo bared her teeth and held out her paws, ready to scrap. Cute, brave, ultimately useless.

"I think we're outnumbered," I muttered, searching for a way out of the tightening ring. Wishing I had something to defend myself. Anything. Not that a single blade would make a difference. I needed a miracle to stomp out the threat. Which led to my lightbulb moment.

CHAPTER

NINETEEN

THE APPROACHING ZOMBIES MEANT I HAD TO ACT QUICKLY. I dropped to my knees. "I have an idea to save us. How would you like to be big? Like really big?"

Mungo blinked those big, jewel-like eyes and squeaked, "Big!"

Enough agreement for me. The problem being, could I find the magic? I dug my hands into the soil, feeling the barrenness of it, and yet as a daughter of the Earth, I knew it could be capable of life. The seed of it dormant until woken.

I dug for that spark, struggling to pull it free, gasping at how hard it was to find even a hint, but once I got hold of the thin thread of magic, I yanked. Yanked and spun that power right back into Mungo.

Magic technically didn't need hexed cupcakes or wafers to work. It just needed shape. Since I couldn't draw what I wanted, I formed the magic via intent.

The goblin-turned-cutesy-furry grew.

And grew.

And grew.

Mungo went from adorable, cuddly stuffy to adorable cuddly *giant* stuffy with enormous feet.

A giggle from Mungo vibrated the air. It caused a shudder to run through the zombies but didn't halt their shambling in our direction. They should have turned and run.

Wouldn't have mattered. An excited, massive Mungo stomped. She waded among the dead, lifting and dropping her feet, crushing heads and bodies like grapes. The eeriest part was not the squish but her high-pitched laughter.

By the time she'd finished, not a single zombie twitched. I'd probably have nightmares for life, but that didn't stop me from hugging the chubby, furry leg and saying, "Mungo saved the day!"

"Mungo!" She beat her chest even as I siphoned the Earth's magic back out. I wasn't dumb enough to have a giant-sized goblin roaming town. It had bad idea written all over it. I shoved the magic I pulled back so hard and fast into the ground, a long-forgotten and crusty seed sprouted and poked from the soil.

I stood, wavering slightly on my feet. Too much magic channeled too fast. I needed to rest. I staggered from the mouth of the tunnel, blinking as I saw two more bodies coming for me.

Niblets! I'd shrunk Mungo before making sure we had a clear exit out.

And I had no juice left to play with.

I hit the ground hard on my knees and broke my fall with my hands.

As my fingers dug in, I felt myself falling as if into a bottomless pit, where I heard someone yell my name...

I woke in a bed. My bed, I should add. I recognized the stucco ceiling with its one yellow spot caused by the nest of rodents in the attic. I kept meaning to paint it.

How had I gotten here?

I pushed myself up on an elbow and glanced around. Everything seemed fine. The sun shone. A glance at the clock showed—

"Nine a.m.?" That couldn't be right. We'd gone to the quarry just past eleven in the morning. Unless... Had I slept an entire day? A stretch of my body said it was certainly possible given how many muscles and limbs popped.

In good news, I'd survived the zombies. Which was when it occurred to me that the two people I'd seen before passing out of exhaustion were most likely my friends. Good thing I'd not sicced anything on them.

Speaking of siccing, where was Mungo? Had she made it out alive? The goblin saved my life, not to mention she was kind of cute. I'd never had a living pet before. Plants were usually my thing. Although I wasn't sure Mungo would think of herself as a pet. But could a human witch claim friendship with a goblin? Why not?

As I sat up in bed—the water under the lily pad leaf rippling with the movement—a glance down showed I wore a T-shirt and panties. Not the ones I'd gone for a swim in. Meaning someone had not only brought me home they'd changed me. The latter, most likely Annie, but the former had to be Reiver. Lovely. Carried by a super hunk while unconscious, possibly drooling. Way to make an impression.

I emerged from my watery bed. The plants in my room shivered and shook their leaves. I made sure to give them a little stroke as I passed them on my way to my dresser, where I found some track pants. I hit the bathroom for a quick refresher before heading cautiously downstairs. More of my inner greenery shook their leaves and stems in greeting as I passed. Nice to know I was loved.

Reiver appeared before I hit the bottom step. "She lives," he remarked dryly. He was more casual than I recalled seeing him before, no boots on his feet, although he did have socks. His shirt was untucked, hair tousled, and his jaw bristly with growth.

Sexy, and to think I'd made out with him. For some reason, the reminder made me duck my head. "Morning," I mumbled. "Thanks for making sure I got home safe."

"Couldn't exactly leave you face planted in the dirt."

My nose wrinkled. "Wouldn't be the first time." Showing off as a teen had led to me passing out in the woods more than once and waking up with a tongue covered in soil.

"You should be careful about how much power

you expend. Losing consciousness like you did could have had a devastating effect."

I rolled my shoulders. "I didn't have much of a choice. We would have died if I'd not acted."

"Because I wasn't quick enough." He appeared angry. Not at me, though, but himself.

"Me being attacked by zombies is not your fault. The important thing is, did we all make it out okay?"

"Yeah."

"What happened after I passed out? The necromancer. Did you find her?"

He shook his head. "There was no one—" He abruptly stopped talking to change direction. "Why did you say her?"

"I met her, the necromancer, briefly, before she doused me in blood to counter the repelling hex and commanded her zombies to attack."

"It's a woman!" He didn't hide his surprise.

"Yes."

"That would explain our difficulty in locating her," a musing reply.

"I'm surprised no one noticed her, because she is quite beautiful." That part still miffed me. Crime wasn't supposed to pay. "Red-haired. Shapely figure. Plotting to take over the world."

"Told you so," was his smart-aleck reply.

I chose to be the bigger person. "We have to find her and stop her."

"Obviously. The good news is you gave us some time. With giant Mungo stomping all those zombies, most likely she'll need to rebuild her army before she can move on to the next phase of her plan. We have to find her before that happens. What's her name?"

"No idea. She didn't introduce herself."

"I don't suppose she dropped a hint about where she laired?" He arched a brow.

My lips turned down. "I assumed the quarry was her base of operations."

"For the zombies, yes, but we found no sign of anyone living there."

Which put us back to square one. I rubbed the spot between my brows. "You haven't said how Annie and Mungo are. Did they get hurt?"

"They're fine. They've gone to fetch supplies. Something about only rabbit food in your fridge."

No meat, nor even some dairy since I'd used it all because of the increase in business at the bakery. "You let them go shopping alone?"

"A public place in the daytime. They'll be fine."

"You sent Annie with a goblin to the store. That has bad idea written all over it." My best friend would literally buy all the candy if the mood hit her.

"I wasn't about to leave you unprotected." A stark statement.

"Why, Reiver, I might almost start to think you care."

He glared. "I'm not a monster."

I couldn't help but throw his own words at him. "You're the one who declared you eschewed personal involvement. Shouldn't your focus only be on eliminating the necromancer?"

"I will. When it's safe to leave you." He ran a finger down my cheek. "It was hard watching you go over that cliff. And then knowing you were alone down there, defenseless—"

"Hardly defenseless. I am a witch, after all." Who'd never managed something on the scale I'd accomplished with Mungo. Had my powers grown? Or had I just never had the need before?

"Yes, you are a fine daughter of the Earth, who gave it her everything. I'll bet you're hungry."

My stomach gurgled as I sheepishly admitted, "Starved."

"Let's hit the kitchen. I prepared some food."

I'll admit I expected he'd offer me meat. A man his size probably ate a good portion of it daily. Which was fine. I just preferred nuts, veggies, and fruits.

To my surprise, fresh cinnamon buns cooled on a plain kitchen plate. I sat down and noted the glossy sheen over the top due to honey instead of icing sugar. My favorite.

"Annie told you of my weakness!" I accused even as I tore a bun free, inhaling the aroma, the spice filling my nose, my fingers digging into the warm dough. I gave it good chomp, sinking my teeth into gooey, sweet perfection. So delicious. It tested fresh out of the oven. By who? Annie definitely didn't bake these.

"Someone's been cheating on my bakery," I grumbled as I ate pure heaven. I could make the best cupcakes and treats in the world, but when it came to anything using yeast? For some reason I failed miserably.

"These didn't come from a store. I made the buns."

I almost choked. Blinking back my tears, I eyed the almost bashful Reiver. "You cook?"

He shrugged. "Why not?"

I opened and shut my mouth, not about to say any of the stupid reasons why. Incongruous it might be, and yet oddly endearing. But I had questions. "How did you make these when I know I have no yeast or honey?"

"I know how to use food delivery."

I blinked. "You ordered groceries?"

"Not exactly. Just the ingredients to make the buns."

"Just." I snorted as I pulled more perfection free. "You might be a little insane."

"My doctor calls it OCD."

That brought a giggle. "At least you're getting help for it. Mmm." I bit into the bliss and groaned. "So good. What else do you make?"

"Mostly bread. I find the kneading calming."

The remark brought my gaze to his hands. A lick of my lips couldn't be entirely blamed on the honey slicking them.

He stared.

"Any zombie sightings while I was asleep?" I asked, licking each and every sticky finger.

"Nope." He shook his head, thumbs tucked into his jean loops. "Nor did we find the necromancer."

"She left after siccing her zombies on me."

"Can you describe her again for me?" This time he took notes on his phone.

"Sure." I went into detail, more than necessary, about her appearance. Then launched into the whole meeting where I sounded much braver than I'd felt at the time.

"A woman," he mused aloud. "It would explain why the CA had a hard time finding a suspect."

"How long has the Cryptid Authority been looking for her?"

"Subject Z, as we've been calling her, started out on the West Coast but didn't get far because of the heat. Bodies decompose much faster."

I blinked. That honestly hadn't occurred to me. "We're not that much better in the summer." But we were heading into fall. The nights were sharp, the daytime not as warm as it used to be, and soon would come the freeze of winter. "How long have you been looking for the necromancer?"

"A few weeks for this one. When they disappear from a location, we have to wait for them to surface."

The familiarity had me asking, "How often do you run into necromancer problems?"

"Usually, not more than once or twice a year worldwide."

"I never knew."

"Because they're usually handled before they can become a problem."

Horror dropped my jaw. "You kill them young?"

He uttered a noise of disdain. "Hardly. When they are a certain age, it is a simple matter to sever their link to the power."

"Oh." A humane way of handling it, even as the thought of being cut off from my magic gave me a chill. "Are they always evil?"

"I'm sure there've been a few who aren't; however, given the troubles the bad ones cause, it's been deemed best to nip it in the bud before it becomes an issue."

"Do you think the necromancer will leave town given what happened?"

He shook his head. "There's no way of knowing. It all depends on if she still needs something here."

"How do we find out?"

"By waiting for the necromancer to make the next move."

"Waiting?" I grimaced. "Doesn't sound like the best plan."

"No shit, but there's nothing else we can do for the moment unless you know where she's lairing."

"There must be a way of figuring that out," I muttered.

"Which will probably take as long as waiting, and I can think of better things to do during that time."

"Like what?" I asked, noticing he'd moved close enough I had to tilt to meet his gaze.

"Given we were interrupted yesterday, we could finish what we started."

He spoke of the kiss. My brain froze. "Um." My brilliant reply before I remembered my promise to myself. "You had your chance to kiss me. No do-overs."

His lips wore a hint of a smile. "You're still angry."

"You basically said I don't matter."

"I say it, and yet apparently don't mean it, or I wouldn't be here."

That snapped my mouth shut. "No one's making you stay. You can leave at any time."

"What if I don't want to?"

"You think I'll be attacked?"

"Maybe." He neared me, enough I could smell soap, my soap, the kind made with a blend of plants that, mixed with his skin, made my mouth water.

"So you're sticking around in case you get to fight."

"No." His hand cupped the back of my head and drew me near. "I'm here because of this." His mouth slanted over mine.

Instant electric shock as our lips connected. The passion of before resurfaced in a way that had me instantly aflame. Needy. Wanting.

His hands grabbed hold of me and lifted me enough he could wrap my leg around his hips and grind against me. His mouth possessed mine in a way that stole my breath and ignited all of my erotic senses.

We might have gone at it hard if I'd not retained the sense to move things somewhere a little more discreet. Not my room—I wasn't sure if my lily pad could handle the pair of us going at it—but I did have a lovely day bed in the tiny third bedroom.

He carried me up the stairs, his lips locked to mine the entire time. The passion between us was explosive. I couldn't have said how or who started the tearing off of clothes, only that we were both naked and falling on the daybed, skin to skin.

My fingers dug into his back when he thrust into me, and I urged him deeper. Harder. Our panting breaths matched as our rhythm found us rocking together, racing for climax.

He grunted when I came, my sex clenching tight and drawing a groan from him as I rode that tidal wave of bliss. I was still coasting on that high when he pulled out, choosing to come on my belly.

Probably should have mentioned I was on the pill beforehand. I appreciated his quick thinking, but that didn't stop me from reaching for his shirt to mop up.

His brows rose. "Really?"

I handed the gooey shirt to him with a curve of my lips and said, "It is yours after all."

His laughter, the first I'd ever actually heard, warmed me but not as much as his touch as he fell on me and rocked my world for a second time.

The third he spent between my legs after a nice hot shower. When I recovered my wits, I was glad to see I'd not torn out all his hair.

Satisfied sexually, I was ready to feed my tummy. "I could use some food."

The suggestion led to him sporting a worried crease on his forehead.

"What's wrong?"

"It's getting late. Annie should have returned by now."

The comment had me forgetting my tummy and scrounging for clothes. "How long ago did she leave?"

"Coming up on four hours. That seems excessive."

Considering the store was less than ten minutes away, even if she did a full grocery shop and hit the liquor store for wine, she should have been done by now. Unless she'd returned and heard us going at it. Knowing Annie, she might have left to give us privacy.

"Give me a second to see if she's replying to texts." I fired off a message. *You okay?*

By the time I finished dressing, there was still no reply. I glanced at Reiver to see him grimacing at his gooey shirt. He wore his jeans hanging off his hips and a strange amulet featuring some kind of horned skull.

I held in a smirk. "I've got something you can borrow." I'll admit I got great pleasure out of seeing him wear a "*Save the Planet. Eat me, not meat* shirt," given to me as a joke by Annie.

He arched a brow. "You can't be serious."

"It's the only thing I've got big enough to fit." I usually used it as a night dress.

He put it on with a scowl, which I softened by getting close and nipping his chin to whisper, "If it makes you feel better, I totally want to eat you."

He dragged me close. "Hold that thought for when I get back."

"Back? Where are you going?"

"To look for Annie and Mungo."

"I'm coming, too."

He shook his head. "I can see you're still depleted. You need to commune with your goddess to complete the regeneration process."

It killed me that he had a point. The glow of sex would do nothing for me if trouble came knocking. I needed to spend some time with Mother Earth to truly juice my inner battery.

"What happened to not leaving me alone?" Maybe I was a little miffed he seemed eager to escape me. Did he regret what we'd done? Wait, did I suck at it? I mean, yes, he appeared to come, but what if it was just a mediocre come and not epic?

"Your home has protection. But just in case, take this." He lifted the amulet he wore and placed it around my neck.

I rubbed my fingers over it, noting the sharp horns on the demonic skull. "Is it magic?"

"Of sorts. It will allow me to find you if you get lost."

"I wouldn't get lost if I went with you." I sounded rather sulky even by my own standards.

He leaned close and murmured, "Trust me when I say I'd rather stay here with you, but you'll never forgive me or yourself if something happens to your friend. Now that you're conscious and surrounded by a source of power"—he gestured to my plants—"you can defend yourself. I'm not planning to be gone long."

"How will you even find her?"

"I have my ways."

With that mysterious reply, he left.

Twenty-minutes later, while I was stress baking cookies, Annie walked in the front door.

CHAPTER
TWENTY

"Holy crap, remind me to never shop with a goblin again! She was constantly running off, putting weird random shit in my cart, and—because of an incident in the toilet paper aisle—might be banned from Walmart," Annie exclaimed as dumped her many packages on my counter while a green-skinned Mungo balanced on her shoulder.

I waved a batter-covered spoon at her. "Where have you been? We've been worried about you."

"Yeah, it took me longer than expected to find everything I wanted. Apparently, there's a meat shortage in town. Becky over at the butcher's says they haven't received any fresh stuff in days because it keeps getting hijacked en route."

I blinked. "Someone's stealing meat?"

"Yup. Had to go to the next town over to find me some bacon." She slapped the package onto the counter, along with a few steaks. But bless her heart, she'd grabbed me meatless chicken nuggets.

"Next town? I thought we were blocked in."

"I know ways of getting out." Annie smirked.

"How come you didn't answer your phone? I tried texting."

"Dead because someone ate the charging cord." Her accusing glare at Mungo did nothing. The goblin ignored her to turn big eyes on me and my batter-covered spoon. I handed it over for a lick.

"Well, because you took so long and didn't reply, Reiver went out looking for you."

"What a sweetheart that man is. To look at him, you'd expect some big, gruff a-hole, but he's got the heart of a hero. And he is totally into you," Annie confided.

"Maybe." Triple sex should have eased my anxiety on that score. Only he'd left, and as I stared at Annie, I realized, "I have no way of contacting him to let him know you're back."

"He's a smart dude. I'm sure he'll figure it out. Now, is that cookies I smell?"

I tried to lose myself in my friend's chatter and the baked goods I couldn't help but make, each one imbued with a hex. After yesterday's zombie encounter, I didn't want to be caught empty-handed.

Zombie-repelling cookies were joined by some pure luck scones and a few reviving nut bars, just in case we wanted to stay awake tonight. We'd crash hard once they wore off, but I wasn't about to sleep knowing the necromancer—and Reiver— remained at large.

Afternoon waned into evening, and still he didn't return. By the time the clock in my living room ticked nine o'clock, I had no doubt something bad happened.

Like he really regretted having sex with me and ghosted. Oops, I said it out loud.

Annie slapped me. Literally, not figuratively. "Don't you start with that shit. The man is besotted with you. Why on earth would you think he'd run off like a jerk?"

"Wasn't it your grandma always saying once a man gets the milk, he has no need for the cow?"

"She also said God invented the G-spot and put it in a stupid place knowing full well men can't find their own ass without help. Reiver didn't abandon you. No way in hell. That man lost his shit when he realized you were in that quarry all alone. And then, when you emerged, covered in blood, I ain't never seen anyone run so fast. Carried you all the way out."

"So what do you think happened?"

"Way I see it, one of two possible scenarios. First, he came across a clue and his dumb ass went looking into it."

"That totally sounds like him." His heroic tendencies wouldn't want to put me in danger.

"Two"—Annie ticked off a second finger—"which might be related to one, the necromancer got her claws into him."

"Don't you mean her manicured nails?" My lips

turned down. "That's actually really plausible, too. She did mention wanting him as part of her evil plot."

Annie planted her hands on her hips. "Are you just going to let her have him?"

"No, but what am I supposed to do? I have no idea where to even start looking."

"Would you rather sit around waiting or actually do something?"

Usually, I had no issue with patience. Cooking required timing and precision. Waiting for certain chemical reactions, internal temp, cooling. But Reiver wasn't a cake. He could be in danger. The longer I hesitated, the less likely we could help if he were in trouble. I shouldn't forget what the zombie puppet mistress said. She wanted to use Reiver, make him her zombie minion. To do so, she'd have to kill him first. I couldn't let that happen.

"There has to be a way of figuring out where he's gone." I paced my living room.

"Do you think they went back to the quarry?" Even Annie sounded skeptical of her suggestion.

I shook my head. "Doesn't seem likely." It occurred to me that while many previous missing residents of the town and farm had been smushed in the excavated canyon, we'd not come across all of them. Including Annie's two horses. Where could they be, and what purpose did the necromancer have for them?

"For some reason my brain keeps circling back to, why here? Why choose our boring town to start her world domination? What do we have that makes us special?" Annie asked, and I opened my mouth to say "I don't know," only to halt.

We did have one company propping up my birthplace. "Crypto Backo."

Annie snorted. "What about them? They're just some tech company offering backup servers for those who worry their hard drives will crash."

"Which means lots of computers. Tons. Processing power galore. Not to mention, all that information."

"Which is encrypted."

"You really think the company storing it can't read it? Information rules the world."

"Why would a necromancer bother going after the world electronically when she can just scare everyone into obeying with a massive zombie army?" Annie's said sarcastically.

This time, I almost gave myself whiplash shaking my head. "That's just it. You could never control the world with fear alone. The necromancer needs actual bodies, decent ones, to act as her soldiers. But we have the weaponry to decimate their ranks. Ruling over a small town is one thing, the whole country? Almost impossible. She can't take over by fighting us physically."

"Then how?" Annie asked.

"Money and secrets make the world go round. Once she takes over Crypto Backo, she'll have the computing power to disrupt not just our nation but the entire world. She can shut down businesses. Drain finances. Pauper entire countries."

"Will she? You're assuming she can get a signal out." Annie argued against my wild theory. Oh, how the cream churned with me now throwing out the crazy ideas. "To foil her plan, they just need to stop the computers, which is easy. They'll shut down the electrical grid to the town."

"Have you forgotten all those new solar roofs Crypto Backo paid to have installed as part of their green initiative? Enough for the whole town plus some." At the time, we'd thought them nuts to do such an expensive thing. Now, it made sense.

Her jaw dropped. "That's so fucking brilliant of them."

"Less admiring, more figuring out how to stop it."

Annie nodded. "Right. I guess since we can't turn off a power switch, we need to block all outgoing signals. What if we cut the fiber for the internet in town?"

"Chances are they're hooked to a few satellites."

Lips turned down as Annie frowned. "Damn."

Damn was right. "Let's start by seeing what we can find out about Crypto Backo."

We immediately jumped online and did a search on the company.

The main website had its propaganda page showing pretty computer sentinels, big black towering cases with flashing lights and the promise of a secure backup of all life's important things. Yet nowhere did I find an actual location of their services other than a vague mention of offices around the world.

Further digging—with Annie accessing public tax rolls—showed that Crypto Backo owned most of the town. So many buildings, some of them still boarded over from the recession left by the defunct quarry. They bought up a bunch of houses, some of them rented to employees. Even the quarry was under their corporate umbrella.

"They own pretty much everything." I couldn't help my surprise.

"Which isn't necessarily a bad thing. We were dead in the water before they stimulated the local economy. Not their fault a zombie queen chose to target them for her plans of world domination." Annie defended them.

"This sounds so crazy."

"Yet it's all true." Annie couldn't hide her glee.

"Doesn't it bother you?"

"What bothers me is we're sitting here while Queen Zombie Bitch is out there making a new army of darkness."

"Let's say she is. Where is she storing them?" She'd need somewhere discreet. "Can you map all the places they bought?"

"Give me a second. I need to batch import a list. Then I assume you'll want it color-coded by type." She mumbled and typed and did things with a computer like I did with my cakes that involved much swearing and swigging of caffeinated cola.

Soon we had a map of the area, with blocks in different colors.

She pointed. "Orange for residential. Blue is for commercial. Green is for uninhabited."

I eyed the various splotches as an idea churned in my head. A nagging sensation had me musing aloud. "What about the horses?" Their disappearance still bugged me "Where could she hide them and not be noticed?"

"Wait, what?" Annie whirled to eye me. "Are you talking about Jeeble and Jumble?"

"I didn't see them in the ravine. Plus, now that I think of it, there weren't enough chickens, either. And where are the other cows? I only saw one."

"Maybe she sent them to her chef?" Annie joked, biting her lower lip.

The answer hit me hard, and I jabbed my finger at the map. "She took them to the train station." The blue blob had railroad tracks running through it.

"You think she's shipping them?" Annie's lips pursed. "Why?"

"Imagine the hysteria that would erupt if zombie farm animals got mixed among actual livestock. People will panic about a zombie outbreak and slaughter anything that comes in contact."

"Why would anyone do that? Zombies aren't contagious."

"I know that. You know that. But think about the media. They'll have everyone believing we're all about to become the walking dead."

Annie grumbled, "What a waste of good meat. But not sure what it will accomplish. Reducing a portion of our meat stock isn't exactly the be-all and end-all. No one will starve."

"The destruction of livestock is obfuscation. While the world worries about the tainting of our food supply, the necromancer swoops in to Crypto Backo, unleashes the power of the servers, and becomes the most powerful person in the world."

"Pretty sure it's not as easy as you make it sound."

When did my friend become the skeptic? "Don't be so sure. I saw it in a movie." Yeah, it sounded dumb even as I said it.

"Speaking of movies, I can get my hands on some explosives," Annie casually tossed out.

"Um, what?"

She grinned. "From when I was blowing up the rock in that new field I prepped last summer."

"How does dynamite help us?"

"Since each building has its own solar panel, we can't shut off power, but we can blow up the locations with computers."

"We don't even know which ones have some. You can't explode them all."

"Not all, silly." She rolled her eyes. "I figure we just need a couple destroyed to throw a wrench in the network."

"What of the people inside?"

Annie had an answer. "We ring the fire bell to evacuate them, duh."

"What if Reiver is hostage inside one of those buildings and can't escape?"

"That would be unfortunate."

A wild shake of my head went with my emphatic, "No. We are not destroying anything."

"Very well. Guess we're hijacking a train then."

CHAPTER
TWENTY-ONE

"Whoa, why are we suddenly hijacking a train?" I asked my best friend, who'd taken my crazy conversation and leveled it up a notch.

"We need to stop the train from running to make sure it doesn't have zombie animals on board." She said that as if it should be obvious.

"Sorry, but I'm not really worried about that. I want to find Reiver."

"And how do you suggest we do that?"

The way literally warmed my chest. The amulet he left me heated and began to glow.

"Why do you have a demon head seething on your chest?" Annie pointed.

I lifted it away from my skin. "I don't know why it's doing that. Reiver gave it to me. Said it would help him find me if necessary."

"A tracking beacon?" Annie brightened. "Can you reverse it to locate him?"

My mouth rounded. "Maybe?" Could I charm it into helping me track down its owner?

Before I could even think of trying, there was a tap at the kitchen window over the sink. I lifted my head to see a green face pressed against it, the bars on the window not impeding the goblin one bit.

Mungo bounded for the counter and over the sink to put its fingers against the glass. She chittered softly, "Friend."

"I think your friend isn't feeling well." As I warned, the goblin bared their fang-like teeth, but it was the milky eyes that freaked me out the most.

"Dead. Not dead." A sad Mungo announcement.

"Sorry, Mungo." I did feel genuinely sad for the creature. It couldn't be easy losing its whole tribe.

Tap. Tap. The goblin on the other side of the glass began slamming into it, harder and harder.

"I think it wants inside," Annie observed as she grabbed the shotgun she'd leaned against the kitchen table.

"What are you doing?"

"Preparing to defend us."

"By shooting up my house?" I exclaimed, my shock more about the actual attack than the fact we would have to defend ourselves.

Crack. The glass splintered.

"Would you like to let it get close enough to hand wrestle?" Annie asked, sliding the pump action to make it click.

"I'd rather—"

Crash. The sound of breaking glass came from elsewhere in the house.

"I think we have company," Annie declared at the scamper of tiny feet overhead.

Before we could react, the kitchen window exploded as Mungo's friend finally shattered the pane. The lithe creature wedged through with no regard for its flesh. It tore and scraped its way in and clacked its teeth. Mungo dropped out of sight into the sink, probably in sad shock.

Annie aimed her gun.

"No, you'll hurt Mungo." I slapped the muzzle down.

The goblin on the sink hissed at me and then uttered the most surprised sound. It looked down at the knife sticking into its body.

Mungo held the hilt and, with a squeal, finished the job. Only when the body split in two did she declare, "Dead."

One down—*crash*—who knew how many more to go?

"Let's get out of here." I scooped up Mungo to ride on my shoulder. On my way out of the kitchen, I snared a bag of treats.

"Shit yeah, grab the goods." Annie grabbed her own stash before she raced ahead for the front door. A good thing she paid attention. Her reflexes had her swinging, aiming, and shooting at the goblin that leaped suddenly onto my stairs. Her aim proved true.

I ignored the hole left in my drywall from the blast. I'd meant to repaint.

We headed outside to my front yard, and I eyed the curb and grimaced. "You brought Tina." Tina being her tiny two-seater dream car. I couldn't have said what the make or model was, not being a car girl. Usually, she kept Tina in the barn, only taken out twice a year for special occasions. Annie claimed it was to preserve it. I said it was because it was an uncomfortable ride.

"I'm not happy putting my baby Tina in harm's way either, but I had no choice. Truck's at the bottom of the quarry lake."

Who cared if Tina left my bum bruised? The ominous rustling in a bush had me moving toward the car. Not even one stride and I saw movement from more plants. Ominous.

"Dead, not dead," Mungo announced as if I needed to know my front yard had a zombie-goblin infestation.

Lithe bodies crawled, climbed, and slyly shifted in our direction, popping their heads out of branches and leaves, hissing as they came into sight.

"This isn't good," I muttered.

Instinct had me suddenly tensing then jerking my leg just in time as the first zombie tried to latch on. Reflex had me punting when it reached for me again. The goblin flew, and I swallowed as the remainder eyed me.

Uh-oh. Bad situation got worse.

Which was when Mr. Leroy emerged onto his porch.

"I called the cops!" he yelled, shaking his fist.

"Get back inside!" I hollered. "It's dangerous."

He ignored my warning. "Now you'll be gone. Wretched witch. Back where you belong. In Hell." Mr. Leroy thumped down the steps, making too much noise.

The undead goblins turned to look at him.

I would have screamed in caution again; however, I could tell by Mr. Leroy's livid expression he wouldn't listen.

The goblins changed direction and aimed for him. I might not like Mr. Leroy, but the man didn't deserve the menace heading his way.

"We have to do something." I reached for my medallion of luck around my neck, only to accidentally grab Reiver's amulet.

"Eat a cookie," Annie suggested.

Zombie-repelling goodie. Of course. I shoved my hand into my pocket and yanked a bag. As I stuffed a cookie into my mouth, barely chewing before I swallowed, I watched as Mr. Leroy finally saw the real threat.

"Get away, varmint!" He started hobbling up his porch steps, only to have a goblin confront him on the top step.

To his credit, Mr. Leroy really could wield that cane. He jabbed, and a goblin died. With the cookie still caking my mouth, I ran for the lagging goblins, intending to stop them with the element of surprise, only to come to an abrupt halt as a feathery bomb dove from the sky.

The crow!

It hit a goblin close to Mr. Leroy and carried it off. It didn't hunt alone.

In the movies, seeing a murder of crows descend was never a good thing. People usually got torn apart, pecked to pieces, killed by beak. Lucky for me—thank you, lucky scone—the birds had a target, and it was small and green.

A smart Mungo hid under my hair lest the attacking crows mistake my live goblin for one of the bad ones. It didn't take long for the birds to remove the goblins while evading Mr. Leroy's wild swipes.

He didn't appreciate being saved.

I could tell the moment the battle ended because the murder rose from the yard in a fluttery dark, undulating wave. It vanished into the night sky a moment before a police car arrived without sirens, just its lights flashing.

"Stall them," I muttered, eyeing the goblin corpses all over the lawn.

I didn't need Annie for that. Upon seeing the officers, Mr. Leroy practically ran in his rush to meet them on the sidewalk with a wild tale of small demons then demonic birds being sent to attack him by me.

Alas for Mr. Leroy, he had no actual bite wounds— blame his own skill with his cane—and the yard didn't hold a single demon body by the time the police deigned to move closer to look.

When the police asked me, "What did you see?" I replied, "Nothing, sir. Did I mention Mr. Leroy has dementia and takes medication?" Which didn't help Mr. Leroy's case.

When Mr. Leroy loudly insisted I was lying, he also unfortunately whacked a cop in the shin with his cane in his vehemence. It led to him getting tucked into the back of a police car to get taken for a mental health evaluation at the hospital.

I waved good-bye when the cops left. Only once they turned the corner did Annie huff, "Fuck me, I'm glad that's over."

As if to mock her, a crow landed on the hood of Annie's car and cawed.

CHAPTER
TWENTY-TWO

THE BIG CROW SQUAWKED AS IT HOPPED IN MY DIRECTION ON Tina's hood, which had Annie moaning, "Not the paint."

"What do you want?" I found myself holding Reiver's amulet, the glow of it intensifying as the bird opened its beak again.

"*Caw.*"

"I don't speak crow."

Follow. The word came from my goddess.

"Follow who?" I asked as the crow flapped its wings but remained grounded.

Birds of a feather flock.

What kind of cryptic nonsense was that?

"Shoo!" Annie waved her hands to no effect.

Meanwhile the crow stared at me, and the amulet Reiver gave me remained hot and glowing. I asked, with quite a bit of skepticism, "Can you take me to Reiver?"

"*Caw.*" It lifted, flapping its wings, hovering midair.

Annie gasped. "Oh, hell yeah. We've got a spirit guide."

Pretty sure that wasn't true; however, I couldn't deny the crow definitely wanted us to accompany it, only we weren't about to go on foot. Good thing Tina could become a convertible. With some heaving and grunting, we pulled the top back to give us a better view of the crow, who circled and cawed impatiently. I noticed the medallion at my neck pulsed with the sound.

"Is it me, or are the two connected?" I muttered, stroking the glowing skull.

"Maybe your guy is like some king of the crows or something."

My nose wrinkled. "Possible, I guess." But it didn't feel quite right. However, I now began to understand how he might have been watching me. Could Reiver see through the bird's eyes?

And had he used that power to watch me undress?

We drove slow enough to keep Mr. Crow in sight. The few times we lost him when he banked around a dark corner, Mungo saved the day by leaning out from my shoulder and pointing until Annie righted our course. We ended up driving right out of town, and a nagging suspicion concreted itself as the crow circled over the train station before landing on the roof of the main building.

Our destination led to Annie slapping the steering wheel and huffing, "Ha, we do have to hijack a train."

I didn't share her excitement.

Emerging from Tina with my butt promising retaliation for the cruelty, I glanced around and saw no sign of life. This time of night, the ticket booth for the few passengers that used its service was closed. The lights on and around the platform shone, every other one only as an energy saving effort. No one waited that we could see. I also didn't see any signs of the missing animals.

A march to the tracks themselves showed not a single car or caboose; however, a large truck was parked nearby, and once we got near, the scent of animal filled the air.

Dead animal that was.

My nose wrinkled. "We're too late." The necromancer had already shipped the zombie farm pets. We must have just missed them.

"That's a bummer." Her lips turned down.

I was pretty sure her disappointment stemmed more from not being able to take over the train.

"I wonder if the necromancer went with them."

"Why don't you ask the birdie?" Annie pointed to the sentinel watching us from the roof.

I clasped the amulet before saying aloud, "Where's Reiver?"

The crow cawed.

Not exactly an answer.

"Lead me to Reiver."

The bird ruffled its feathers and didn't budge.

"Could he still be here?" I mused, turning to glance around as if I had a super gaze that could pierce darkness.

"If he is, then where? This place is deserted."

"Inside the station?"

"Maybe?" Annie didn't sound convinced.

A yank of the doors to the main building showed them locked. Peeking through the glass, I saw no one inside.

"Now what?" I exclaimed in frustration. It didn't help my goddess hadn't spoken again. Even putting my hand on a stubborn weed—determined to grow in the harshest of places between the cracks of cement on the platform—provided no guidance. I didn't receive any orders or clear vision of my next move.

Moving away from the station, I craned my neck to eye the roofline, only to realize I'd lost Mr. Crow.

"Poop on a stick," I vehemently cursed.

"Ooh, listen to that language." Annie snickered. "Someone's mad."

"I feel helpless, and I hate it," I grumbled.

"More like someone's miffed she doesn't get to play the witch to the rescue to her handsome hunk," Annie teased.

"Not miffed so much as worried. I don't want anything to happen to him."

"If it will make you feel better, I've got the bombing equipment in the trunk. Betcha blowing up some of those Crypto buildings will draw the necromancer's attention."

"You mean we've been driving around with explosives this entire time?" Eyeing Tina's tiny backside, I remembered the jostling. The thumping. Maybe I'd walk home. "We are not blowing up any buildings." I remained firm on that score.

"Are you sure? It might be the only way to stop the zombie queen."

"That's puppet mistress, actually," drawled a lilting feminine voice. "And it's already too late."

CHAPTER
TWENTY-THREE

WHILE OMINOUS MUSIC PLAYED IN MY HEAD, I WHIRLED TO see the necromancer had snuck up on us, looking especially cute in her white silky jumpsuit and loose-knit shawl. Her hair was layered in red waves over her shoulders. Her lips painted a matching vivid hue. Her scarlet heels made her almost as tall as Reiver.

Yes, Reiver, who stood by her side, blank-faced. He was also dressed in white—button shirt, trousers, and slip-on loafers with a white sports jacket, looking utterly preppy and respectable–probably screaming inside his vacant head.

"What have you done to him?" I yelled.

The necromancer smiled. "Made him into my perfect pet."

"You killed him?" I said in a soft, horrified whisper. He didn't look dead, but then again, his body would be fresh.

"Actually, he's still alive since I have a different use

for him. I like the big, virile types. They're much more fun to break." She ran a finger down his bulky arm, and he didn't react one bit.

I, on the other hand, saw red and green but mostly raging red. "You're horrible."

"What will you do about it?" she taunted. "Bake me a cake as fast as you can?"

"Die, evil bitch!" Annie chose to pump her shotgun and aim. Brave, but not well thought out. If she fired, she might hit Reiver. I knocked into her, jolting her aim.

The gun went off, and Annie cursed. "What are you doing?"

"You'll hurt Reiver."

"Your man is gone! Death to the zombies," Annie yelled, waving her gun.

"He's not dead, just under her spell."

"Then he might as well be dead, cheating fucker!" Annie remained staunchly on my side.

Meanwhile the necromancer laughed. "Such an amusing pair. But I don't have time for this. Tonight, I begin my takeover of the world."

"Oh no you're not," I grumbled.

The zombie puppet mistress smirked. "And how will you stop me? I don't see an army."

"I don't see yours either. Oh, that's right, we stomped it into gooey submission," Annie sassed right back.

The necromancer appeared too confident by far. "Who says I came alone?" She didn't move. No snap of her fingers. No stamping of her foot or zombie call required to bring the shamblers in sight. They came from around the train station, across the tracks, and soon made a mockery of our rescue plan.

"How? I destroyed your army," I said.

She snickered. "Bah. What you fought were the leftovers that I had no real use for anymore given their stage of decay or general uselessness." Nice to have her declare I'd made absolutely no difference. "As you can see, I've already drafted new soldiers."

A study of the bodies showed them mostly dressed in office wear. Wanna wager which company they used to work for?

"You won't get away with this." My threat was completely baseless.

"I already have. As we speak, my hackers are in place, taking over the Crypto Backo servers. My pets are on their way to causing chaos. The only thing left to do is celebrate. Right, my sweet angel man?" Her smarmy smile didn't elicit a response from Reiver.

But it got one from me. "I won't let you hurt him."

"Oh, what I have planned for him won't hurt. You, I'm afraid, are about to wish you'd stuck to baking pies and cookies."

The only positive? "Your zombies can't see me," I stated, knowing better this time than to get splattered by blood.

"No, they can't, but your friend can."

"What?" I asked with puzzlement as I was shoved from behind. "What the heck?" I whirled to see Annie about to shove again, her expression glazed, as if mesmerized. "Annie?"

"Annie's not home." A singing statement followed by a giggle. "Have fun getting killed by your best friend. I'm off to celebrate my domination of the world!" The puppet mistress uttered a chilling cackle as she left with my lover.

The ring of zombies tightened as my best friend lifted her shotgun and fired!

TWENTY-FOUR

Something of Annie must have still been in there because she missed—unheard of. That or I moved fast enough.

"Annie! Wake up," I shouted. I hit the ground just as she fired again. Mungo sprang from my shoulder and bolted. Couldn't really blame her.

Click. Click. Annie kept firing, but she'd run out of ammo. I doubted she'd keep dry shooting for long. I had to act.

The zombies pulled tight, as a noose looking to strangle, with us in the center.

"Annie, you need to wake up." Then again, maybe it would be a kinder mercy if she never saw the clacking teeth as they bit into her.

I clutched the amulet. "If anyone is listening—crow, the bogeyman, god of whoever this belongs to—I could use some help."

The carving warmed in my grip, enough it became

uncomfortable. I released it with a gasp, but the amulet got hotter. I yanked it from my neck and held it away from my body.

Which was when the crow swooped from the sky, snatched it, and flew away.

"Schnizzle sticks," I huffed.

Now what?

I ducked Annie's wild swing. She must be fighting the compulsion because we both knew in a fight she'd kick my tushie.

The concrete all around had only loose dust and grit, marred by a single crack with the scrubby weed.

One tiny stubborn plant. A plant that meant life and a connection to my goddess.

I dropped down to my knees and touched it, the tenacious weed with its roots spreading deep into the ground.

Mother. I need your help. Please.

I begged, and she replied not with words but action. Magic jolted through me, enough of it my lips parted on a gasp. The power of life itself filled me, just in time.

Annie swung the empty gun at me, knocking me aside, but I hummed with energy and grabbed the barrel before she could smack me again. I yanked it from her grip and tossed it aside before lunging for Annie.

Ever see those charlatans play healer? They slapped a person in the forehead and yelled, "*I heal thee in the name of God!*"

Me, I clung to Annie's calf with both arms and sobbed, "Please, snap out of it. Please. Annie." My plea came with a push of magic that coursed into my friend, and she froze. Stood still enough I dared to crack an eye and look upward. "Annie?"

She glanced down at me. "Oh. Shit. Thank fuck I missed."

"Annie!" I popped to my feet to hug her, but she didn't squeeze me back for long.

"Um, Mindy, we have company."

I'd been trying to forget about the zombies in the hopes they wouldn't see us. After all, we'd eaten the hexed cookies.

In one respect, they did ignore us. They certainly didn't reach for us, but they kept drawing closer and closer, their final order obviously to congregate in a tight knot, with us in the middle.

"How are we going to get out?" I asked, looking for a gap in their bodies and finding none.

"Can you fix them like you fixed me?" Annie asked.

"Probably not."

"Why not?"

"You weren't dead."

"But they are. Can't you remind them somehow?"

How did one explain to the dead to lie down and behave?

One couldn't, but I might be able to do something about the string keeping them animated.

"Watch my back, I'm going in." I darted for the closest zombie, a woman in a cardigan, long brown skirt, and sensible shoes. She looked like a mom, one who'd never come home to make a meatloaf dinner again.

I slapped my hands to her cold cheeks, ignored her moving jaw, and focused. The sense of wrongness almost overwhelmed. Death. Decay. Darkness. I almost recoiled. Puke roiled in my belly, but I held on until I found what animated her, the spark inside her head that falsely ordered the body around. A spark of life, trapped, that wanted nothing more than to escape.

Freedom.

I pulled the nugget of life free. The body dropped, ripping from my grip.

"You did it!" Annie exclaimed. "Only forty-nine more to go. Give or take."

As if I'd have the strength to free so many. But I didn't have to do them all, just enough to get us out. "Stay close," I warned as I created a path.

By the third de-animated zombie, I'd figured out how to quickly get in, yank the spark out, and move on. I did my best to not cringe as I stepped over and sometimes on the bodies that collapsed onto the ground.

We made it clear of the zombies but kept going, leaving them behind. They didn't try to follow. Thank goodness for the repelling cookies.

I dropped to a crouch, panting.

"You okay?" Annie asked, a hand on my back, rubbing in a soothing circle.

"Nothing a cleansing bath won't fix," I lied. It would take me a while to forget the vileness and wrongness of what I'd just done. The taint of death perverted into something evil clung to me, a miasma that would require immersion with my goddess at the muddiest level to erase.

"What now?" Annie asked.

With us out of the thicket of zombies, we had a choice to make. Hide or fight?

I straightened. "Now we blow some shit up."

CHAPTER

TWENTY-FIVE

Unfortunately for my friend, I didn't actually plan to level any buildings. It occurred to me we couldn't let the zombies on the platform wander. They might appear like a shuffling nothing burger right now, but their taste for human blood made them dangerous.

Since I couldn't be sure I'd find the necromancer, they had to be handled—aka permanently killed—which led to the dilemma of how to remove the spark from that many at once without getting our brains chewed on. This was where Annie's dynamite, in a crate marked simply "Danger," came in handy. She pulled it out of Tina's trunk with care.

I ogled the metal box with its skull and crossbones above the warning. "Where did you get that stuff?"

"I know people."

"Do they work for ACME?" I asked sarcastically.

"You going to help or mock?"

She flung open the lid to show thick padding on the inside. She handed me a stick. I felt like a certain coyote before explosive death, yet I had no other plan.

We tied fuses to the five rods and quickly ran them in a ring around the zombies who thankfully continued to ignore us. It felt like we wasted hours of time, but by the time we were done, and I was checking my watch while Annie cursed her lighter that wouldn't light, I realized less than fifteen minutes had passed.

Fifteen minutes plus how much more since Reiver left with that hag? Pretty on the outside but rotten within.

"Aha!" Annie succeeded in getting a flickering flame and lit the fuse. We watched with our arms linked, waiting for the kaboom.

It was more like a kersplat. The bombs went off around the dead bodies, and the impact exploded them. I shrieked and ducked a flying head, but Annie got bitch-slapped by a spinning arm.

The rain of meat chunks quickly stopped and even before the smoke cleared, I knew we'd managed to rid ourselves of the threat.

"Time to go before the cops show up." She flipped around and marched to Tina, opened the driver side door, and squealed as a head bounced out and landed on her feet.

Annie put a hand to her mouth. "I think I'm going to puke."

"Don't puke on—"

Annie spewed, but rather than on the ground, spattering the head staring up at her, she puked sideways, into the topless Tina.

I gaped at our ruined ride. "Gross."

Annie hiccupped. "Sorry.

"You do realize another few seconds and the head would have been gone. Vomit is forever."

"I know. My poor seats," she lamented. Because she didn't just throw up; she sprayed.

The zombie mess vanished on its own, the puke did not. We could only do a quick clean of the bile-covered cookie goo in her car. Could have been worse. Anything with a red sauce never came out.

"We really should get going." Annie kept eyeing the road outside the parking lot. There was nothing residential nearby, and yet someone might have heard the blast.

"But where?" I mumbled, getting into the car and trying not to breathe deep.

The car shifted into Drive, and as Annie drove, the air got better. "Where would a crazy zombie lady go to celebrate world domination?"

"We don't have a fancy hotel since the Luella burned down." Supposedly kinky sex gone wrong, that was the most common story. The sub tale being it had to do with a pair of cryptids doing magic they shouldn't have. Rumor further claimed that the CA ordered the place torched to destroy all evidence of what they'd done.

"Maybe she borrowed a house on Millionaire Row." Not the actual name of the street where the poshest houses in town hid behind stone walls and gated entries.

"Possible, but how would we ever know which one?" We couldn't exactly start knocking on all the doors. Reiver didn't have that kind of time.

Annie slowed to a stop and glanced at me. "You want me to just drive around and hope we find him?"

Before I could reply, she whispered, "What the fuck is that?"

I glanced in the direction of her pointing finger. Something swooped toward us, oddly shaped, lumpy, with wings. Maybe some kind of bird? Or—

The crow landed on Tina's hood, and Mungo waved from its back. The goblin hadn't abandoned us at all but rather gone after the crow.

More astonishing were Mungo's next words. "Find. Man. Lead."

"Wait a second, are you saying you found Reiver?"

Mungo nodded. The bird stamped its clawed feet.

"You smart, adorable creature." I wanted to hug Mungo, scaly skin and all. "What a brilliant idea. You've saved the day by finding out where Reiver is. I'll be making you so much cake when this is over," I promised.

"Cakey!" Mungo beamed, a terrifying, yet somehow endearing thing. "Go! Lead," Mungo declared and gave a tug to the bridle it had created by wrapping the stolen pendant around the bird's neck.

How she'd come to wrestle the amulet from the crow and use it to conquer it? No idea, but I would have loved to watch.

"*Caw.*"

The crow pushed off of Tina's hood, leaving scratch marks that had Annie screeching, "I'm going to bake you in a pie!"

Not if it helped us save Reiver. At least now we had a direction. We followed the swooping bird for the second time that night, driving the quiet streets of town until we ended up in front of an old church. Saint Judas, here since the town was founded in the late 1700s, a thing of stone, multi stories high, with a bell tower and a cross that often attracted lightning. The surface of it was covered in a vine long dead and dried. Bought by Crypto Backo. I remembered the scandal around the time it happened.

Mr. Crow landed on the Virgin Mary's marble head. Mungo hopped off and tugged the amulet free, keeping it wrapped in a little green fist. "Here."

I eyed the dark building askance. "Are you sure?" The church doors had been sealed for years, the chains around the handles rusty and untouched.

"*Caw.*" The crow ruffled its feathers.

Mungo marched up the steps and pointed. "Man."

The confirmation had me getting out of Tina to get a closer peek. "The door is blocked. We need another way inside." How had the necromancer entered? Perhaps a rear entrance?

I sidled around the side of the building, Annie

huffing at my back. A glance over my shoulder showed her carrying a pesticide sprayer with a nozzle and her lighter.

"What's that?" I pointed.

"Homemade flame thrower. Learned how from the internet. I've got like a mixture of gas and stuff in the tank. Light it and whoosh." She pretended to torch everything.

"You're going to die young and make me sad, which will lead to me overeating, no longer fitting in my favorite jeans, and getting depressed."

Annie uttered a long-suffering sigh. "You ruin all my fun."

"By keeping you alive."

"Whatever," she grumbled. "Wait here while I get my axe."

Axe? How many weapons had Annie brought? And a better question, exactly how much trunk space did Tina have?

I kept moving along the side of the church, bordered by empty parking spaces, aiming for the rear. All places, even of worship, had more than one way in or out. As I turned the corner, I halted.

I'd found Annie's horses, bearing saddles adorned in flowers and ribbon. It might have been cute if not for their chewing on someone's innards. *Slurp.*

Gag. I slapped a hand to my mouth, keeping the cry and vomit inside. Too late for the horses. They weren't the only protection.

A pair of people, still dressed in their work clothes,

held guns and vacant expressions. Zombies didn't use weapons, meaning I'd finally found living minions. No one mentioned necromancers could control minds. Or was this puppet mistress a breed heretofore unknown?

Since I couldn't gain entry without a possible bullet wound or becoming a zombie-horse meat-treat, I returned to the front of the building, running into Annie and her axe on the way.

"Where are you going?" she asked, pausing with her axe leaning over her shoulder. It worked with her outfit: plaid shirt and overalls. No holiday theme today.

"To see if there's a better way in." Perhaps the far side held another entrance.

"You found zombies? Want me to take a whack at them?" She slapped the haft into her palm.

"Don't go back there." I wasn't about to tell her the foals she'd raised were slurping on intestines. "There are guys armed with guns."

"Shit." Her lips turned down, only for a second. "We'll have to go in the front. I'll get the bolt cutters."

I almost asked her why she even had any in her car to start with before deciding I didn't want to know. Her preparedness would come in handy. "That would be great." And probably noisy. But what other choice did I have to get inside?

Mungo tugged at my leg, and I reached to scoop her, placing her on my shoulder. "I don't suppose you know a way in that won't draw attention."

"Ding." Mungo pointed.

The answer made no sense until I glanced upward to the tower where the bell hadn't rung in more than thirty years. The last time had been the start of the scandal that led to the downfall of the church.

My lips pursed as I eyed the distance. "Great idea. Only I can't fly."

Annie returned with massive bolt cutters that might have been cousins to the jaws of life. "Why fly when you can ask that ivy to help you?" A casual suggestion as she sauntered to the door, ready to jingle our presence to the world.

"Can't talk to something that's dead."

"Is it dead? Or just hibernating?" Annie knelt to clip.

I eyed the barred church doors, remembering how when I was little my mother dragged me here Christmas Eve for mass. The only time we ever went to church, and it was, to be honest, kind of special. There'd been something pure and beautiful about the choir singing and emerging from the church just after midnight to a crisp, wintery night, often with fresh falling snow, soft lights, and the knowledge Santa had been by and left me presents under the tree while I wrecked my knees praying, wondering why my mom always made me wear a skirt. Given the time of year, I'd never actually gotten to know the young ivy only starting its twining journey up the stone.

Annie proved quieter than expected, and no one

came to investigate. While she worked on the lock and chain, I neared the gnarly leftover vine clinging to the church, dry enough it would crack if I even so much thought about climbing it.

Mungo had no such trepidation, grabbing hold and scurrying quickly upward. The plant had taken over after the church closed due to a scandal involving our pastor, six married women, and twice as many bastards, leaving us without someone to guide the flock. His last orgy was forever commemorated by the clanging of the bell as Mr. Ferguson, one of the cuckholded husbands, rang the pastor's head off it. The pastor recovered and was reassigned. A replacement was never sent.

The church shut its doors and nature had taken its course. The ivy might have fully overtaken the old structure if not for the drought two years ago. People who watered their yards and gardens kept their plants alive, but those plant without caretakers... Only the hardiest survived.

While I'd done my best to bring water to the needy, I'd not been able to save them all.

I put my hand on the stripped, dry bark left behind. *I'm sorry.* I'd never even thought to come by and check on the old church property.

To my surprise, I felt a glimmer of life. Just a tiny one. Deep, deep down in the roots of the ivy, named–

"Lazarus. Nice to meet you." I'd never met the ivy during its woken phase before. My brief Christmas visits had been during its hibernation time. Given its age, it had achieved sentience, though, and could still communicate, apparently.

The bark under my hand shivered. Something agitated it. Probably the dead people bothering its home.

"You don't like the zombies. Me either."

"Aha!" Annie pulled the chain free, the cloth she used muffling the rattling of metal links. "Get ready to kick some ass." She hefted the nearby axe as she pulled on the doors. They swung open to show plywood had been nailed over the opening from the inside. "Seriously?" she yelled.

I couldn't rebuke her, not while she experienced such frustration, but I did cringe as she swung that axe at the plywood. *Thunk. Thud.*

So much for the element of surprise. We wouldn't have long now that she'd drawn attention.

The vine under my hand writhed. It couldn't speak, but it could make me feel and understand. It offered a suggestion that took my glance upward.

I shook my head. "You're not strong enough." Not currently, but I could give it strength if my goddess listened. The ivy's roots went deep. Deep enough I could send a plea.

Mother.

No need to even ask. She filled me with her blessing. Glorious power and life. I didn't keep it for myself but thrust it into Lazarus.

For a second, I thought I'd killed the ivy. It went completely blank. Then a mighty tremble rumbled through it, shaking all the leaves, shivering the vines. It helped that the sky chose that moment to rain, giving moisture to a plant long parched. With the magic and the water nourishing it, Lazarus returned to life.

TWENTY-SIX

THE VINE PLUMPED AND LEAVES SPROUTED AS MY GODDESS kept channeling her will through me. The ivy returned to its former glory, stronger than ever.

Smart, too. It twisted around my waist and snaked upward, bringing me to the window of the bell tower and depositing me gently inside. I gasped, not just because of the surprise but also the loss of connection to my goddess. We no longer communed, but her blessing coursed inside me.

The interior of the bell tower held leaves and dust, empty beer bottles, cans, and wrappers. Also Mungo, who peered down the stairwell.

"Any zombies?" I asked.

She nodded. "Dead. Not dead." She held out her green clawed paw. "Cookie."

Might be time to re-up the magic, just in case. I ate one, and Mungo, unlike the last time, contained herself to one as well.

"Ready?" I whispered. I knelt and held out my hands for her to step into, only Mungo shook her head. "Spy." With that one word, she scrambled down the steps

I followed cautiously, the shine of the moon outside not extending to the dark stairwell. I didn't dare create any light. It would only pinpoint my location. At least my arrival was muffled by the thudding of Annie and her axe.

Using fingers trailing on the wall as my guide, and careful steps, I made it to the main level and a closed door. I almost screamed as Mungo muttered, "Dead. Not dead."

Zombies on the other side. Probably going after Annie, who'd slowed down her chopping.

I peeked through to the next room, the entrance vestibule, large enough for about a dozen or so people. It held a tight wad of bodies, groaning and shoving, wanting to get at the moonlight gap in the plywood covering the entrance. Only one could push through at a time, but would it still be too much for Annie?

Should have known my friend had a plan.

"Come and get it, fuckers!" Annie chortled. A second later, I spotted flames. The torching of the zombies who made it outside didn't deter the rest.

With them distracted, this was my chance.

I slipped into the church proper, still lined in wooden pews, the stone floor dusty. It was illuminated by candles spread around the chamber, their flickering flames enhancing the shadows. The altar where the pastor used to preach was covered in a black swath of fabric and, standing by it, the necromancer and Reiver, wearing only his pants.

About to be defiled. I'd arrived just in time.

"Unhand him!" I shouted.

"You again." The necromancer sighed. "You're becoming bothersome."

"Good. Because evil should never be easy."

"Are you for real? Everyone knows being bad is the easiest, and the badder you are, the better the results."

"That's crazy talk."

"That's real world, cupcake girl. It's why people like me will always win over people like you," she sassed.

The nerve. I advanced. "I won't let you hurt him."

"What I have planned won't hurt one bit." Her lascivious smile roiled my stomach, and I would have sworn Reiver flinched.

"You're not touching him." It occurred to me I didn't have a weapon, but neither did she. I ran, yelling, only to stumble as a sharp stab of pain in my head took my breath and blacked out my sight for a moment.

What's wrong with me?

The poking diminished the more I focused, and I realized why when the necromancer whined, "How are you blocking me?"

I wasn't about to admit I had no idea. "Because I'm stronger than I look."

She snorted. "Doubtful. You'd think the angel would have been the impossible one to breach."

"What angel?"

The necromancer's lips quirked. "You didn't know? This hunk of a man is an angel."

I blinked and glanced at the shirtless man with slabs of muscle, no wings, and definitely no halo. "Reiver?" Yeah, I had my doubts about that given I'd heard him cussing more than once.

"Yes, him. He's a Nephilim, half angel, which means no wings or divinity but lots of strength and morality. Such fun to corrupt."

"Won't you make the angel god angry if you hurt one of his, er, grandchildren?" How did one refer to them?

Her laughter rose to the peaked ceiling. "God abhors the fact his angels have base desires and act upon them. If given the choice, he'd wipe the earth clean of them."

"Oh." Meaning no one to save Reiver but me. I could do this. The necromancer didn't have her zombies this time.

Before I could decide between putting up my dukes or ploughing into her, the necromancer said, "Kill her."

It took me a second to realize who she commanded.

The only other person with us.

Reiver came at me without question, and I dodged his slow stalking while rapidly babbling. "Now, Reiver, you know this isn't you. We like each other. A lot. I think. Hard to tell since you don't say much and—" I ducked his sudden lunge and ran, huffing, "I'm sure you would rather not kill me. Eek." I hit the floor as he tackled me, his heavy weight pinning me. "Reiver!"

Yelling his name did nothing. The poor man wasn't in control. I bucked and fought, which only resulted in my being on my back, looking into his beautiful eyes— the terrible blank eyes—as he put his hands on my neck to squeeze.

He's going to kill me.

I tried to do as I had with Annie. Put my hands to him and tried to sever that link.

It worked.

For like all of three seconds. Then the necromancer had him back in her control.

I severed the compulsion again.

And again.

And...

It proved jarring to watch his expression go from horrified to blank as he choked me. It wouldn't be long before my magical well ran dry and the stone under my fingertips and body had nothing to give.

Where was my goddess when I needed her?

Right here.

I heard Mother speak but couldn't find her, as my eyesight grew dim.

Look deep.

I thought she meant look in Reiver, but there was nothing in him that belonged to my goddess. My head turned to the side, and I saw the necromancer's ankles, blurry with my dimming vision. I reached anyhow, weakly wrapping fingers around them.

The evil woman laughed. "Ah, the dying throes. My favorite. And then, the resurrection as my tool."

The idea of becoming a zombie horrified. I was dying. I'd soon be undead. How horrible. How–

It was then that I felt it, a kernel inside the necromancer. A seedling potential waiting for the right kind of conditions to flourish.

I reached for it and gave it my last dying piece of magic before I passed out.

TWENTY-SEVEN

I WOKE, WHICH I'LL ADMIT WAS A NICE THING TO HAVE happen. Last I recalled, Reiver was choking me and the necromancer was cackling her victory.

Then... I'd thrown my last bit of magic at her. I guess it worked since I lived. A hand to my throat showed it intact. I wasn't at home. I didn't recognize the room I found myself in; however, I did know the long leather coat hanging over the chair.

Reiver. He'd not killed me. Had he snapped out of the necromancer's control and come to his senses in time?

"You're awake." He entered the room softly and eyed me with, dare I say, a hint of trepidation.

"Yeah, and kind of surprised by it. What happened?" No soreness in my throat or raspy voice. I realized nothing hurt.

"How much do you remember?"

"You choking me out."

He winced.

"I know that wasn't you."

"Yeah, but I couldn't stop. And trust me, I tried." He grimaced.

"She had you dancing like a puppet."

"Did you take Zoey out?"

"Is that her name?" I'd never actually heard it. Seemed kind of innocuous for someone trying to rule the world.

"Yeah."

"How did you find her?"

"After I left you, looking for Annie, I found Zoey a few blocks from your place, exactly as you described. Then again, I would have recognized her anyhow since she emerged from a building with a bunch of fresh walking dead. Thought she'd be easy to take out."

"Only she grabbed hold of your mind."

"Didn't even know that was possible." Pure annoyance in that admission. I didn't add to it by saying it didn't work on me. "Anyhow, next thing I know, rather than taking her head, I'm being led around like a puppet, aware but unable to act." His lips turned down. "A good thing you arrived when you did."

"How did you break free?"

"I didn't. You saved us. Zoey apparently had a left-over popcorn seed stuck inside her. When you commanded it to grow, it practically exploded out of her."

The description caused me to wince. "I didn't know what else to do."

"Your fast thinking is what saved the world. Once she died, all her compulsions wore off, and just in time. The hackers she had taken over never finished the job."

"And Annie?"

"Still insane. But in a good way," he quickly added. "She was the one to advise me to lay you in a nearby patch of tall weeds so your goddess could heal your wounds."

It explained why I felt great.

"Mungo?"

"Is fine as well, although she did take off after the final showdown. Annie seems to think she'll be back."

I had no doubt the goblin would because I owed it a cake. I was morbid enough to ask, "What plant popped out of the necromancer?"

His mouth lifted at the corner. "Corn."

It made sense. "Probably wedged in her intestine somewhere because of diverticulosis." To think, if she'd had proper medical attention, I might not have gotten so lucky. "I can't believe we stopped her in time and saved the world."

"Not we, you. And quite honestly, I'm just glad you got there before she could complete her plan." He shuddered.

"I'm sure it wouldn't have been that bad. She was very attractive."

That led to a grimace. "Not on the inside she wasn't. I like my woman kind of nature and smelling of cookies."

"Oh, you do?"

He grinned. "I can show you if you'd like."

"I should probably check in on Annie." She'd been my friend too long for me to ignore her for the throbbing in my pants.

"Annie is fine and currently enjoying room service at my expense on another floor."

"That will be expensive," I warned.

"Worth every penny if we get the night to ourselves."

We got until dawn. We made good use of those hours, taking a shower together, which ended in him trying to drown as he made me come with his mouth on his knees. Then in bed while indulging in a midnight snack. I might have gotten wake-up sex if not for a goblin staring at me from the pillow when I blinked open my eyes.

"Mungo? Hi."

"Cakey." The goblin patted my cheek.

"I'm glad you're okay." I truly was.

As for Mungo... "Hungry." She grinned, and so did the friends she'd brought along.

EPILOGUE

THE NECROMANCER'S PLOT TO CONTROL THE WORLD FAILED. Reiver received a commendation for his actions from the Cryptid Authority, and despite being at a career high, he retired.

To make bread. With me.

Given we'd be churning out twice the goods, we expanded the bakery into the building next door and hired a few people to work for us.

Annie's insurance company balked but, in the end, offered her enough to buy new animals. She also expanded her operations to keep up with demand. With the zombie livestock scare, people were wanting to go back to the farm and have a more direct line with what they ate.

The number of zombie hoaxes that popped up afterward lasted a while. Not everyone wanted to believe a necromancer was needed to make them.

People claimed to have been bitten and craving flesh. The scamming lasted until the vampire scare that hit New York and stole all the headlines and trending hashtags.

Annie, a smart businesswoman, started growing garlic, which we then used in Reiver's coveted garlic-parmesan bread crosses. They sold like crazy, not only because of their hex by me to foil the blood-sucking undead but they tasted beyond heavenly, probably because my boyfriend was half angel. We'd had a chat about it once I'd had enough sex to last me a few hours.

"The necromancer said you're a Nephilim?" I stumbled over the word.

He'd shrugged. "Yeah. It's not a big deal."

So he said, but I made a point to never scream, "Oh my god," during sex.

Ours was a partnership made on Earth, not Heaven. They weren't kidding when they said Nephilim were persona non grata, which amused my goddess to no end. I think she purposely tried to irritate the other god by making flowers spring up whenever Reiver walked barefoot on the ground.

My very own hunter, baker, and happy homemaker. A fairy tale ending for a witch.

THE END OF A STORY INSPIRED BY A BEAUTIFUL COVER. BUT I AM LEFT WONDERING...WHAT ABOUT ANNIE? SHE'S GETTING HER STORY NEXT IN EARTH'S LAIR.

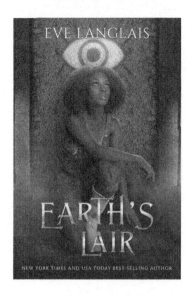

For more Eve Langlais books visit EveLanglais.com